ALL IS NOT FORGIVEN

BOOKS BY JOE KENDA

NONFICTION
I Will Find You: Solving Killer Cases from My Life Fighting Crime

Killer Triggers

FICTION
All Is Not Forgiven

ALL IS NOT FORGIVEN

JOE KENDA

**BLACK
STONE**
PUBLISHING

Printed in the United States of America

First large print edition: 2023
ISBN 979-8-212-52871-9
Fiction / Mystery & Detective / Hard-Boiled

Version 1

Blackstone Publishing
31 Mistletoe Rd.
Ashland, OR 97520

www.BlackstonePublishing.com

I dedicate this book to my wife, Kathy;
our son, Dan; and our daughter, Kris,
who have shared what has turned out to be
a rather remarkable and extended ride for
a kid from Pennsylvania coal country who
spent most of his career hunting killers
in the foothills of the Rockies.

PROLOGUE

Dear Reader,

This book marks a departure from my two previous books, **I Will Find You** and **Killer Triggers**. Like my reality television shows **Homicide Hunter** and **American Detective** (on the Investigation Discovery and discovery+ networks, respectively), those books featured nonfiction accounts of true stories drawn from my case files as a patrol officer, detective, and homicide detective lieutenant with the Colorado Springs Police Department from 1973 to 1996.

This book in your hands, however, is a work of fiction. The story and its characters are made up, mostly. I say "mostly" because this story was inspired by a case that I worked on as a rookie detective. That case never became public because much of it remains a mystery. It still fascinates and haunts me, so I wanted to share some of it with you in fictional form.

The narrator of this work of fiction is yours truly, but the main character is my fictional self as a much younger detective circa 1975, which is when this tale begins. I have resisted the temptation to make myself better looking, or smarter, or with the abs of an action figure hero.

All the other characters in this book, both good and bad, are fictional beings, though more than a few also were inspired by people, or canines, I have worked with, investigated, come across, or learned about over the years.

And, finally, there are many unusual, horrifying, and remarkable stories told within this book. As a police officer and homicide detective for more than twenty-three years, I can assure you that while none of them are exactly true, none are beyond the realm of possibility either.

Please keep all of this in mind as you read, and I hope you find the experience interesting and enjoyable.

Detective Joe Kenda
(retired), 2023

CHAPTER ONE

CLUB APHRODITE

MONDAY, JUNE 9, 1975
COPENHAGEN, DENMARK

The killer was not an emotional sort, yet he felt a twinge of nostalgia as he walked past the entrance to Tivoli Gardens on his way to the brothel and a meeting with his favorite forger. He had been to the amusement park as a boy visiting from Germany, though he could not remember which foster parent, court-appointed guardian, or child molester had brought him.

He was only nine or ten at that time, and his recollections from that visit, as well as those from most of his childhood, were willfully buried and walled off. The memories stirred on this day were of a much different visit to Copenhagen's landmark tourist attraction. His fondest remembrances, twisted as they might be, were from his activities within the park only five years ago.

This was in the summer of 1970, when he was still a member of the federal police special forces stationed near Bonn. Bored out of his mind with the constant training exercises and lack of real action, he had come to Copenhagen for the kind of thrill not offered within Tivoli Gardens. Sexmesse was a weeklong sex fair, a trade show for Denmark's flourishing pornography industry with more than fifty thousand smut vendors, perverts, and voyeurs from all over the world.

I normally prefer gun-show porn, but this is a very close second, he thought upon entering the high school gymnasium hosting the event. There, he joined the lustful stream of gapers, which was 99 percent male, mostly middle-aged, and desperately unattractive.

So many wankers! There is no way in hell I would visit the restrooms here. I'll piss myself first, he thought.

Topless go-go dancers were stationed at most of the booths. They hawked vibrators, whips, riding crops, leather corsets, masks, and stiletto-heeled shoes, many of them in men's sizes. A large, obese, bald man pitched male potency pills at a booth made to resemble an erect penis.

Why would a man hoping for a stiffer cock buy something from an ugly man who so closely resembles a pecker himself?

The killer lingered only at a booth featuring several tables of S&M books, magazines, photographs, and posters. He was drawn to the most violent images, which matched those that played out in his thoughts, dreams, and memories, beginning in childhood.

His mind had wandered back to the locked closet where his mother kept him during her meetings with clients, but those memories were interrupted when a husky voice called out, "Hey, you, the handsome one, come talk to me. Maybe we can do business."

It was one of the go-go girls, but this one had beard stubble and a hairy chest. Six feet tall with every exposed inch of skin covered in prison tattoos. A barrel of ink lost. The aggressive vendor was waving a giant dildo that flopped like a dead python. The killer formed his right hand into a gun, aimed for the head, and pretended to pull the trigger.

Go-go guy backed off.

A short time later, the killer left the Sexmesse event, both disgusted and aroused by its degeneracy. He walked to the red-light district behind Copenhagen Central Station in search of a prostitute. He chose an Asian girl, not for her beauty but for her small stature. Like most of the other girls on the street, she was forced into prostitution to work off her debts to the sex trafficking gang that had "liberated" her from a village in Laos and brought her to Copenhagen.

The killer noted this without sympathy. His capacity for empathy had been drained at an early age. Life treated him cruelly and he responded in kind. And so, he drugged the tiny Laotian and raped her throughout the night in a hotel room just a few blocks away from Tivoli Gardens. While she was still drugged and unconscious with her wrists and ankles tied to the bedposts, he slit her throat with his Bundeswehr combat knife, a souvenir from his days with the GSG 9.

After placing her body in the bathtub, he went to work cutting her to pieces with a pair of short bolt cutters like those used in most morgues. He took his time, admiring how the cutters went through bone as easily as tissue. The following night, he packed just her small torso into a laundry bag and then dumped it in a trash bin. He waited for Tivoli Gardens to close for the night before placing her severed body parts in his hiking backpack. He entered the darkened park by easily scaling a fence.

While distributing the prostitute's body parts in a manner designed to maximize the horror of those who discovered them, he recalled reading that Walt Disney had been inspired to create his own idyllic theme park in the USA after a visit to Tivoli Gardens.

It is a good thing Mr. Disney won't be here tomorrow to see what I've added to the attractions, he thought.

A BAD FIRST DATE, JULY 1970

Niklas Larsen, fifteen, could not believe that the most beautiful girl in his class, Trine Pedersen, had accepted his invitation to go to Tivoli Gardens.

"Is this a date you are asking me on, Nik?" she teased.

"Ha! I would never ask you on a date, you nerd!" said Niklas.

He had loved her since the seventh grade when he sat behind her and spent every day staring at her thick blond hair and dreaming of taking her around the world on romantic adventures.

Niklas was a rare Danish male, a bookish romantic who was infatuated with just one girl. Trine had been slow to appreciate his charms. Through most of **folkeskole,** Trine had kept Niklas on friend status while saving her affections for older boys. She thought of Niklas as a nice but somewhat strange guy, who read travel books and watched foreign movies for the scenery. She did enjoy talking to him, especially since he didn't try to grope her like most other boys.

Then, that summer before their final year in **folkeskole,** Nik grew out of his awkward adolescence and Trine began to see him differently. Now, she found him interesting and attractive as well. So, when he asked her to go to Tivoli with just him, not the usual gang of friends, she accepted.

This may be our first date, even though I won't let Nik know I see it that way, she thought.

They met at the entrance to Tivoli Gardens just as the park was opening for the day. Nik already had their admission tickets in hand, but Trine insisted on paying him back.

"I am a modern Danish woman, after all!" she said. "We pay our own way."

Nik accepted without debate.

"Our first ride should be the Rutschebanen, the antique roller coaster," he said. "It's been my favorite since I was a little kid."

"You are so uncool, Nik, and that is why I like you!" said Trine.

There was only a brief wait in the line before they boarded their wooden car behind the brakeman. Nik flushed when Trine pressed her body against his. They both laughed as the coaster clattered away on the wooden rails from the boarding area and entered the first series of drops and curves.

On the first slight drop, Nik felt something brush against the calf of his left leg, but he was too distracted by the delighted screams of Trine to pay any heed. When their coaster car pitched forward on an even steeper drop, he again felt something heavy bump his calf. This time, he lifted his leg and foot slightly, and out from under the seat rolled a woman's severed head.

Trine and Nik screamed together in horror at the sightless eyes and congealed blood. They were still shrieking when the roller coaster ride ended, and their voices were part of a greater chorus of terror. Throughout Tivoli Gardens, tourists from around the world were screeching in horror after discovering severed body parts covertly disbursed by the killer.

The prostitute's hands had been tied around the pole of a carousel horse, placed low near the saddle. A Swedish couple failed to notice them before placing their five-year-old son Finn on the carousel horse. He touched the hands before seeing them. His shrieks marked the beginning of a lifetime of nightmares and ghastly visions.

Minutes later, an American soldier on leave and his German girlfriend discovered the prostitute's legs and feet when they took seats in a car dangling on the Ballongyngerne Ferris wheel. Their outraged cries were heard just as an elderly couple from Tokyo jumped into the lake in front of the garden's Japanese Tower after finding the prostitute's breasts stashed on the seat of their small motorboat.

The chaos that ensued throughout the park forced the closing of Tivoli Gardens for an entire week, a rare occurrence in its history, dating back to 1843. Police identified the victim as a Laotian prostitute after a monthlong investigation but they found no trace of her deranged killer. The European press called him "the Tivoli Butcher."

PAPERWORK

Looking back on those events from five years earlier, the killer thought, **Ahh memories! I gave that hooker the final rides of her lifetime.**

He looked once more upon the twinkling lights of Tivoli Gardens, drew a deep breath, and savored the cool night air before stepping into the back entrance of Club Aphrodite, an entirely different place of amusement.

Inside, four hookers in various stages of undress were smoking and drinking coffee in a break room. They did not look so appealing in the harsh light, but it did not matter. He was not there for pleasure.

An off-duty Copenhagen cop moonlighting as a security guard was with the hookers on their break, hoping to score a freebie. When the stranger entered through the back door, he put down his cup of coffee and reached for his revolver, then thought better of it when the fierce-looking intruder stepped into the light and glared at him.

They don't pay me enough to get into it with that sort. Whatever he is after, he can have it, the security guard thought.

The killer noted the guard's decision to back off and nodded to him.

Wise move, he thought.

ABBA's "SOS" throbbed faintly in the back hallway but was blasting from the built-in speakers at
the front of the building where the club's main business was conducted. The killer paused to admire a
young woman who approached and then slid past
with her eyes downcast.

A new girl? She seems submissive. I like that.

Raven-haired and naked to the waist, she was so
beautiful the killer wanted to capture her image and
hold on to it, but she moved too quickly by him.

I will have to remember to ask about you, he
thought.

While still transfixed by her image, he came to
an unmarked door inside the labyrinth. He paused
a second, clearing his thoughts, reminding himself
of the purpose for this visit.

The killer had learned of the forger's services
during an investigation that was part of his past life,
his legitimate, boring law enforcement job. Since
leaving his government position for more exciting
and better-paying work, the killer had been in this
room on several occasions. **I can trust him, at least
one more time**, the killer thought, before knock-
ing on the door.

It was opened by a small, stooped man with a jeweler's loupe in one hand.

"Good afternoon, Herr Ernst."

"Yes, hello, Herr Schmidt, good to see you again. Please come in."

The killer stepped in and then stepped back. He'd forgotten about the damned cuckoo clocks.

Tick, tick, tick, tick, tick, tick, tick . . .

The forger's workroom was packed wall to wall with the maddening, tacky, damned clocks.

Does he keep them running so his customers don't stay long? If so, it's working on me.

"I am going to the United States, and I will need the usual papers," the killer said.

"Where do you want to base this identity?"

"Chicago area, the state of Illinois."

That's all you need to know, thought the killer.

"Do you have a name in mind, or should I provide one?"

"Please, you choose, but not any I've used previously."

"I understand. I already have your photo on file, so your American passport and driver's license will be ready in three days. You can pay then, since you are a repeat customer. Will there be anything else?"

The killer was already out the door, eager to escape to ABBA and "SOS" in the hallway before the damned clocks struck the hour and all cuckoo hell unleashed. He had planned to return to Germany that evening, but the encounter in the hallway with the new girl inspired a change in his plans.

He did not turn right to exit the building. He turned left instead, moving down the dark hallway toward the blaring music and the brothel's reception area.

"Welcome back, Herr Hecht," said Madam Steinau, who ran the brothel. "What is your pleasure today?"

"I believe you have a new attraction, whom I saw in the hallway a few minutes ago," he said. "Dark hair, quite stunning, and submissive in her manner?"

"Yes! Roma was recruited by our Russian talent scouts. She is lovely, cleared medically, fit, and yes, very eager to please."

"Is she available for me, now?"

"I believe so, she was on her break when you saw her in the hallway. Now, Herr Hecht, I will ask that you be gentle with her because on your last visit the girl took some time to recover. So, with that in mind, I must also ask that you post a substantial damage deposit along with Roma's fee, which I hope will encourage you to take your pleasures without inflicting injuries on our precious new girl. Do you agree to those terms?"

The killer bristled, not at the demand for additional deposit so much as the attempt to place limits and controls on his desires and methods for fulfilling them. He briefly considered walking out. He could find other women at lower fees with fewer restrictions within a few blocks. Most of them would never be missed. They were expendable. Yet, none were as alluring as this Roma. She might become a habit, if she was at all cooperative.

"I will play nicely," he said, forcing a smile and producing a thick wad of American cash, the preferred currency.

"She did mention seeing a very handsome and fit man in the hallway when she returned from her break," said Madam Steinau. "I told her you were one of our most valued customers."

"Thank you," said the killer. "I promise, she will incur no serious injuries from me."

Madam Steinau froze at his words and the tone of them.

"Herr Hecht, we have an agreement. If she is injured in any way, serious or minor, your deposit will not be refunded, and you will be blacklisted. Our Russian friends may seek their own penalties, as well."

The killer did not fear Russian mobsters, nor did he care about losing the deposit. There were other brothels in Copenhagen and throughout the world. Yet, he believed this Roma was worth preserving for future encounters, so he did not argue.

"What about a little bruising, is that permissible with this girl, Madam Steinau?"

The hostess extended her palm.

The killer placed an additional $5,000 in her hand.

"I am certain you will enjoy your evening, Herr Hecht. Ahh, here she is now."

The killer turned and nearly collided with Roma, who had quietly entered the room as the transaction for her services was completed. The killer took pride in being ever alert to his surroundings, but her stealth startled him. She stood so close, he had to step back to take in her striking transformation.

Roma had changed into a black leather dominatrix outfit, a series of straps supporting a see-through mesh bodysuit that bared her breasts and crotch. She carried a matching black leather riding crop.

Her demeanor had changed to match her outfit. She was no longer in a submissive mode.

"Madam Steinau! Might there be an additional fee if my services were to include my bruising of Herr Hecht as well?" she asked. Her six-inch stiletto-heeled leather shoes allowed her to look down upon him, enhancing her power position.

"Why yes, there would," the madam said. "I could even join you if Herr Hecht wanted double the pleasure and double the fun!"

"Thank you for your offer, Madam Steinau, but I believe Roma will be more than enough woman for me," he responded without humor.

The killer handed over another $5,000 in cash as his dominatrix fastened an iron collar around his neck, giving the chain attached to it a good yank before leading him to her chambers.

Mesmerized, he followed without protest.

At last, a woman after my own heart.

CHAPTER TWO

THE GUN SHOW

FRIDAY, JUNE 27, 1975
DOUGLAS COUNTY FAIRGROUNDS
CATTLE AND HOG EXHIBITION BUILDING

Castle Rock Gun Show
Friday, Saturday, Sunday
$5 Admission

The killer, posing as Terrance James Schumacher, 41, of Joliet, Illinois, drove into the parking lot of the Douglas County Fairgrounds in his Budget rental car, a 1974 Ford LTD, secured with cash. Herr Ernst's expertly rendered state of Illinois driver's license had passed the test at

Denver's Stapleton International Airport just an hour ealier.

Colorado's largest gun show had opened its doors just a few minutes earlier, so the Cattle and Hog Exhibition Building was not yet packed with people packing heat. This was perhaps the only event held at the Douglas County Fairgrounds that did not discourage an open display of weaponry.

The killer found it ironic, then, that a sign posted at the entrance said, "Strollers must be checked."

I see that in this part of the world, guns don't kill people, baby carriages do.

Humor was not his forte, in any language. He was a deadly serious man, a requirement for a predator in his specialized field, and today he was in search of a specific weapon for his next contracted kill.

"Happy hunting!" said the cheerful lady who took his five dollar bill at the front entrance and then stamped his hand with the emblem of the National Rifle Association, an eagle atop a shield and two rifles with crossed barrels above the date 1871.

Gun shows in America, the land of the free, are a boon to those in my business.

They are not simply "gun shows," of course. They are open markets where weapons are offered for sale or trade. No identifications or permits are required for transactions between private sellers and buyers here, which meant no traceable paperwork. In the killer's native country, the only thing more difficult than purchasing firearms is obtaining a license to carry them.

The man posing as Terrance James Schumacher thought, **God bless America. The only weapon you cannot legally own in this country is a nuclear weapon.** He'd heard of a German who came to the US and bought a Panzer IV tank with an operating cannon and two mounted machine guns from another collector. **What fun it would be to drive around these mountains, picking skiers off chair lifts like ducks on a pond.**

Even the killer's random daydreams involved violent death, and worse. For him, the gun show was like a farmers' market for a chef. All the fixings were on display. There were more than eight hundred vendors manning six long rows of booths and tables loaded with guns, rifles, shotguns, automatic weapons, ammunition, knives, brass knuckles, machetes, and other weaponry.

The smell of gun oil blended with the acrid scents of manure and urine left by the cattle and hogs that were auctioned off for slaughter in the same arena the previous week. The musky odors and milling crowds of gun enthusiasts added to the livestock show atmosphere, the killer thought.

So much beef on display, these overfed Americans, and so many posing like GI Joes and Dirty Harrys, wearing camo pants, T-shirts, and hats from their NRA. I doubt that any of them have ever shot a human target except in a video game. I could probably wipe out the lot of them with a couple blasts from an Uzi.

He noted that couch commandos and special forces wannabes vastly outnumbered those who appeared to be serious hunters, collectors, or sportsmen. Most of the males were beneath contempt. The women, at least the younger women, were more interesting to him. Some were strolling arm in arm with partners, male and female.

Many of the single women appeared to be trolling for johns, flashing enough bare breast to invite public indecency charges. Three or four of the youngest and sexiest caught his eye as worthy of his attention.

Perhaps later.

He was dressed to blend in: muted colors,

suburban wear off the discount racks at the local mall. Brown leather bomber jacket, khaki shirt, and brown slacks. Only his black running shoes were from an upscale brand. The dirty blond hair beneath his black cap was close-cropped military-style.

A careful observer might note his broad shoulders, slim waist, lean musculature, and confident bearing. Predators cannot easily mask their nature. He spoke quietly, with a faint European accent, when he stopped at a booth displaying the revolver he'd been seeking. The booth was manned by a scrawny, bearded, and pony-tailed fellow wearing a Vietnam Veteran ball cap and a T-shirt bearing an image of a double-barreled shotgun pointed at the world. The redundant caption below said, "I support the 2nd Amendment."

The killer gave him no eye contact and instead scanned the revolvers spread out on the table. He selected a Smith & Wesson K-15 in blue steel with a four-inch barrel and a six-round capacity. He knew the history of this 1960s weapon, which was standard issue for US Air Force pilots and crews.

He checked the trigger and the timing of the cylinder with an expertise that the vendor rarely observed in his gun-show customers.

"Yes, sir, that is a fine firearm," the vendor said, sniffing a potential sale. "Well made, completely reliable. Had it for years. From my private gun safe."

The killer paid him no heed. He held his finger up to the bore and looked down the muzzle, using his fingernail to reflect the overhead light and illuminate the interior. **Lands and grooves appear normal with little wear.** He locked the cylinder closed and checked it for play. **The trigger feels crisp and unaltered.**

"This will do," he said.

While the pleased vendor removed the price tag from the revolver, the killer picked up a box of Remington target ammunition from the table. An unusual choice, it might seem, but chosen with purpose.

"Yes, sir, I figured you for a target shooter. You can put them all in the ten-ring and paint one over the other," the vendor said.

The killer raised an eyebrow, waiting for a price.

"Yes, sir, I can let you have the gun and the ammo for, let's say, two hundred dollars. If you pay cash, of course."

Cash is king at gun shows, and the killer was all about leaving no paper trail. He did not haggle.

He peeled two one hundred dollar bills off a roll produced from his pocket. The vendor bagged the revolver in its original box along with the box of ammunition. Transaction complete.

The killer surveyed nearby tables, dismissing the superfluous jewelry stands and booths peddling survivalist gear, military medals, war surplus rations, and a vast selection of testosterone pills and energy boosters.

Scanning a few rows down, his eyes fell upon a familiar weapon, a Heckler and Koch MP5 thirty-six round 9mm. He went to examine it. The German-made submachine gun, one of the world's most popular tactical weapons, appeared to be only slightly used.

This table's vendor was young, dressed in a faux paramilitary outfit. He wore sunglasses inside the arena, so the killer assumed he was an idiot; an opinion quickly validated.

"That is semiautomatic only," he said.

Not really, the killer thought. **It takes only a minor adjustment to the sear to make the transformation that I would need.**

He caught his own image reflected in the idiotic sunglasses and raised an eyebrow.

"Twelve hundred, cash," said the moron.

Impulse shopping was never so lethal, the killer thought. **This weapon might prove useful one day.**

The vendor held the German weapon at eye level to make certain he had removed all the price stickers and tags before bagging it.

As he accepted the package, the killer noted that his purchase had drawn the attention of someone he had noticed earlier. He'd seen him walking with another man, scanning the crowd as if they were looking for someone. Now, he was positioned at a booth two rows away, near the table where the killer had made his first purchases.

Strangely, this fellow stood at a booth that featured women's jewelry, and the vendor was ringing up a purchase the man had made. He seemed to be in a hurry. He was the younger, shorter of the two men who'd caught the killer's eye earlier. They did not fit in with the rest of this crowd. This one was dressed in a cheap blue suit and tie, and wearing rubber-soled dress shoes like those favored by law enforcement. The other with him—older and much taller—had on a Western-style suit, cowboy boots, and cowboy hat. They were clean-shaven with short haircuts.

Both had bulges in their coats, indicating that they were wearing shoulder holsters.

The killer had made them out to be local law enforcement, possibly detectives looking for a suspect, maybe with the government agency regulating firearms sales, or, possibly, the FBI. This younger one, dark hair, blue eyes, had been studying the killer while he purchased the submachine gun.

"Schumacher" weighed his options. A shootout inside a gun show was not an appealing prospect given that probably 98 percent of this crowd was armed. If this cop or agent reached for his holstered weapon or came toward him, he would move quickly into the thickening flow of people and head to an emergency exit he'd noted earlier. Grabbing a hostage was another option, but that would slow him down and complicate things.

"Hey, Kenda!"

The killer heard the taller man call to his associate now standing in the aisle a few booths down. The taller one pointed to a scruffy, pale man in ill-fitting clothing who was talking to a vendor near a display of cheap handguns. The younger cop turned and walked swiftly to his partner. They had a brief conversation before approaching their apparent target from either side, grabbing his arms, cuffing him, and walking him toward the exit.

This eased the mind of the killer. He took his purchase and moved to the other side of the building, turning back in time to see the cops walk their catch out the door and into the parking lot.

So, it seems I was not the person they were interested in after all. That young cop probably just wondered what I'd need this weapon for, but he didn't have a chance to ask. My good luck. Let's see how far it will take me today!

He signaled to a dark-haired woman strutting alone around the perimeter of the sales floor. She was marketing her own wares, without a doubt; braless, blouse barely buttoned, micromini skirt, and stripper heels that brought her height to nearly five feet.

A tall woman would have been nice for a change, but short women are just easier to dispose of.

She followed him out the door. They negotiated her per diem price next to his rental car. He paid her cash up front, one thousand dollars American for four days and four nights of companionship in an isolated mountain cabin he had rented outside Colorado Springs.

She opened the passenger door and got in. The killer drove off with her.

Well, this day has gone even better than I'd hoped.

CHAPTER THREE

A DISMEMBERED HAND AND A MEMORABLE CASE

SUNDAY, JULY 6, 1975

I was just starting out as a detective in the Homicide division of the Colorado Springs Police Department in 1975 when my partner, Wilson, and I were sent into the Rocky Mountain foothills to pick up a severed hand. Stray body parts weren't all that unusual in my line of work, but we would eventually connect the rotting appendage to another case that would prove to be the most complex and far-reaching investigation of my career.

As we dug into this case, we hit a series of remarkable twists and turns on a trail that became very crowded with suspects, lawmen, and assorted sordid players scattered around the world.

Back then, as it was unfolding, I was so green I didn't have any frame of reference about the strangeness of this investigation. I kept wondering, "Are they all going to be this crazy?" As a rookie detective, I did not have a lot of perspective. I was still a sponge soaking up every bit of tradecraft available to me.

Fortunately, our homicide lieutenant had paired me with a veteran, Det. Lee Wilson, who was smart, tough, and mostly tolerant of a twenty-nine-year-old eager to prove himself. Wilson was a street fighter with an artistic side. He'd been a gravel-voiced singer and lead guitarist in a Nashville band in his younger days. Word was that he'd had to give up playing gigs after demolishing a bar. The main problem was that he used four hecklers as his sledgehammers.

My brawny six-feet, five-inch partner humbly downplayed the bar fight story.

"Naw, I hardly touched those fellers. I had to quit because my wife threatened to leave me if I didn't get off the road. Besides, she wanted to move back to Colorado to be closer to her family once she finished up at Vanderbilt's Medical School," he said.

I looked up to Wilson. He pretended that I was

a pain in his ass, but I figured he was just practicing his version of tough love. He taught me a lot, but then, I had a lot to learn.

THE HAUNTED HIKING TRAIL

On our way up to the foothills to collect the severed hand, Wilson informed me that bodies and random human bits and pieces often turned up at our destination, the hiking trail known as Gold Camp Road. The trail followed the original railroad between Colorado Springs and what was known as "the world's greatest gold mining camp," which operated near Cripple Creek in the late 1800s.

The original rail line from the mine followed a path that a flea might take on a hot griddle; plunging, leaping, and zigzagging for thirty-five miles through mountain tunnels and canyons at ten thousand feet above sea level, which is four-thousand feet higher than Colorado Springs at the other end.

In the 1920s, part of the old rail route became a paved toll road popular with tourists. The views are spectacular. President Theodore Roosevelt once trekked up there and hailed his hike as "the trip that bankrupts the English language." Locals debate whether Teddy was referring to the challenges of expressing the natural beauty of his hike, or whether he meant there weren't enough words to describe the terrors, ghouls, and haunted mountain tunnels encountered along its path.

Over the years, there have been many tales of hikers and campers who've come down from Gold Camp Road unable to speak and driven to the edge of madness by what they've seen. Some claim they heard screams from immigrant railroad workers trapped when the tunnels collapsed on them during construction in the 1800s. Others have reported seeing blood stains on the walls of the tunnels, and ghostly images that fade away as you approach them.

"It's the only trail in Colorado that should be marked by signs saying, 'Warning, be wary of falling rocks, large predators, rattlesnakes, goblins, demons, and ghosts,'" said Wilson as we drove.

I told him that my daughter had gone hiking up there with some of her friends and, for weeks afterward, she'd had nightmares from the horror stories she heard.

"One of them was about a school bus full of kids being buried when one of the tunnels collapsed. She swears they heard crazy screams and laughter coming from the closed tunnels," I said.

"I saw a story the other day quoting a local psychologist who said the horror stories associated with Gold Camp Road might be due to some form of mass hysteria," Wilson said. "I've seen enough crazy real shit up there that it gives me nightmares too. I've had to investigate a dozen cases of bodies and parts of bodies found along that trail. Sometimes I wonder if a damned disposal company dumps medical waste from hospitals and morgues up there."

"When I was a patrolman I had to check out a severed head that had been brought home and left on the porch of a guy who lived just off Gold Camp Road," I said. "The dog was pretty proud of itself too."

"That reminds me, the canine unit is bringing three search dogs to hunt for more body parts," said Wilson. "Odds are that the voluntary mountain disposal team has already done a number on whatever else was up there by now."

"What's the voluntary mountain disposal team?" I asked, walking right into Wilson's trap.

"Bears, mountain lions, coyotes, vultures, among other of God's own cleanup crew," said Wilson, who liked to think of me as a city slicker even though my childhood romping grounds was in the Pennsylvania mountains.

HAND OFF

We made it to the trailhead parking lot where we met up with the couple who'd found the severed hand. They were waiting with their dog and Trooper Maurice "Moe" Birckhead, a Colorado state patrol officer, who'd been in the area and responded to their 911 call.

K. C. and Jane Ellen Lafflin from Littleton, Colorado, had been hiking below Pikes Peak along an 8.6 mile unpaved section of the trail overlooking Colorado Springs to the northeast. Their relaxing Sunday stroll abruptly ended when their golden retriever, Smokey, did what retrievers are born to do.

"Jane, what's Smokey carrying?"

"Probably some old bone or stick."

"Smokey, come here!"

"Oh, Jesus Christ! It's a hand! Jane, it's a goddamn hand!"

"I'm gonna puke. It smells so bad!"

"There's a payphone in that hikers' shelter. I'll call 911!"

Another tale of horror was about to unfold on

the old mining trail where so many ghost stories began and ended.

Sgt. Birckhead had placed the severed hand in a bag for picking up dog shit. The dog kept eyeing it and then looking at me. Maybe it was hoping for a reward.

"We'd heard all the stories about the old tunnels on this road being haunted and full of strange things, but I gotta say, we never expected to find something like this," said Mr. Lafflin, as the state trooper delivered the doggy bag.

"If you've got this, I'm out of here. This area creeps me out," said Sgt. Birckhead.

As he walked away, three El Paso County Sheriff squad cars pulled up.

"Looks like we're gonna have a party," said Wilson.

Three county deputies exited their cars and walked over to us.

"Hey, city boys," said Deputy Rick Davis, who moonlighted as a musician and sometimes jammed with Wilson in his garage. "We heard you might need a hand. Oh, wait! I see you have one already."

"Ha! Cop humor! Good one, Ricky," said Wilson. "I think you are out of your jurisdiction, but if you want to join the search that might give us a leg up."

The three deputies found that hilarious. Jane Lafflin was not amused. She buried her face in her husband's chest. It looked as though she might toss her cookies.

"Seriously, Wilson, do you want us to call out the El Paso County Search and Rescue team?" Deputy Davis asked.

"Naw, we only use them if we're looking for a live person who is lost or missing. I don't think that's what we've got here," Wilson said. "Besides, with all the critters out here, this hand could have been picked up ten miles away and then dragged or dropped where the Lafflins' dog found it. So, we're just going to do a quick look with the canines rather than call in a bunch of people."

"Yeah, okay. Well, maybe we'll hang around and see what your dogs dig up," said Davis.

"Suit yourself, it must be a slow day in El Paso County," I said.

Just then, three canine units pulled up. The Lafflins' golden retriever lost its mind, barking like a maniac.

"Smokey!" yelled Mrs. Lafflin.

"I'd suggest you leash your dog before they bring out the search team, otherwise, their handlers might have a hard time keeping them from tearing ol' Smokey to pieces," said Wilson.

My partner wasn't a dog lover. As big and tough as he was, Wilson was terrified of the police canines due to a childhood encounter with a pit bull that took a chunk out of his thigh and nearly neutered him.

"Kenda, you get the Lafflins' statement, I've got to take a piss," Wilson said to me, shambling off to a porta-potty in the parking lot.

The chief canine officer and trainer, Joe D. Gregalunas, waved to us and went to the rear of his SUV to release Vom Glock, the alpha male. The German shepherd, a savvy veteran of many searches, hit the ground and stuck its nose in the air to get a good first whiff of his surroundings.

The next canine out of the vehicle was a younger male, Fonto, my personal favorite, a German shepherd built like a Sherman tank. Fonto and I had a bromance that sometimes got us both in trouble.

"Fonto!" I said, even though I knew better than to treat a police dog like a pet.

"Dammit, Kenda, now you've got my canine unit slobbering and whining like a frickin' poodle," said Officer Gus Amm, a supersized former marine drill sergeant who'd grown up on a Midwestern farm and could have pulled a plow by himself. Gus was moved off patrol duty into the canine unit because he was the only guy strong enough to keep Fonto in check.

We were joined by Officer Kristi De Palma who was doing her best to hang on to the leash of her canine, Diego, a Belgian Malinois that looked like it could eat an entire buffalo in one sitting.

"Hey, De Palma, why don't you just put a saddle on Diego and ride that beast?" said Wilson, always the tease.

"Hey, Wilson, how 'bout I unleash this beast and let him snack on your gonads!" replied De Palma, who was one of eleven Sicilian siblings, the only female, and took no shit from anyone.

"Okay, enough snappy banter," said Officer Amm. "Kenda, if that's the hand in the doggy bag, bring it over here and pull it out so our dogs can get the scent."

I'd already put on my crime scene gloves so I wouldn't leave any prints on the hand.

"I'm gonna barf again," said Mrs. Lafflin, staggering toward a steep drop-off.

"Sorry, guys, she teaches Catholic elementary school kids, so I thought she was tougher than this," said her husband.

Fonto and Diego took turns sniffing the hand and filing the scent away in their dog brains. Officers De Palma and Amm then split up, taking their canines in opposite directions down Gold Camp Road, allowing them to wander off if their noses took them somewhere.

While they did their jobs, I took my first close look at the severed hand, which wasn't nearly as decomposed as it smelled. Wilson walked up and joined the examination as I turned it over a couple times.

It was obviously a woman's hand, small, with nails that had once been neatly manicured. There were marks where rings had been.

"Holy shit, Kenda, look at the ink stamp on the back of the hand!"

Dirt, dried blood, and bruising covered most of it, but I could see that Wilson was pointing to what appeared to be a faint tattoo of some kind.

"Looks like an eagle and a couple rifles . . . I'll be damned. It's the same NRA stamp that we got at the gun show last week!" I said.

Wilson and I looked at the back of our own hands, where the faint outline of the same ink stamp was still visible.

"They change that hand stamp every day at that gun show, so the victim must have been there on the same day we were there to nab Buckler," said Wilson, referring to the prison escapee we had tracked to the convention. "That's just too frickin' weird that we might have seen her there, and then her killer cut her up and dumped her body parts up here."

"Of course it's weird. All the weirdest shit happens on Gold Camp Road," I said.

CHAPTER FOUR

A CLEAN HIT

SATURDAY, JULY 12, 1975

Kathryn Montgomery had just returned home from a Saturday night dinner with her ladies' group at the Spires Country Club. On the short drive from the clubhouse to her home off the first fairway of the golf course, she heard a disturbing news report on her car's radio:

"Colorado Springs police were called to Gold Camp Road this afternoon when a hiking couple's dog found a severed female hand. A police canine search was conducted, but no other body parts were found. Police said they will continue to investigate, but Detective Joe Kenda said identifying who the hand belonged to will prove difficult without additional evidence."

Kathryn prayed silently for the victim and her family and then, as she pulled her Mercedes into the five-car garage, she thought, **Well, thank goodness we live so far from that area where so many bad things seem to happen.** Though sleepy from three glasses of French pinot noir, she put off going to bed to prepare the cash payments for the gardener, the lawn service, the pool guy, and the cleaning lady, all of whom would return to work on Monday wanting to be paid.

Now I won't have to do this before my appointment with the money managers to sign the papers creating that new trust they've been pushing. I'll be glad to get that done since we've been talking about it for a year.

That thought led to her reaching for the phone mounted on the kitchen wall to call her husband, Fred, who was in Las Vegas for a "business meeting." She put the phone back down before dialing.

Why bother? He'll be at a casino somewhere, losing money and getting drunk, or worse.

Kathryn Montgomery was standing at the kitchen counter at the rear of the house, mulling the idea of pouring a nightcap when, unnoticed by her, the lock on the front door silently turned.

Minutes earlier, the rental car leased to Terrance James Schumacher of Joliet, Illinois, had parked on the street at a far corner of the two-acre Montgomery property in The Spires, an affluent country club community in the foothills overlooking Colorado Springs. A ten-foot hedge blocked sight of any activity on the street from the fourteen thousand square-foot, seven-bedroom French country estate home with panoramic city, golf course, lake, and mountain views from all three levels.

The lean driver of the rental car, clothed in black down to his running shoes, walked two blocks away from the car and the Montgomery home, surveilling the area for pedestrians, drivers, private security, street lighting, police vehicles, and anything that might disrupt or interfere with his plans. He then returned to the car and again scanned the area, making certain that no one was watching him from the shadows or the street.

By now, most of these wealthy arschlochs **have retired for the night or they've fallen asleep in front of their television sets after consuming too much alcohol.**

He had already spent three days monitoring activity in the Montgomery home and surrounding neighborhood. His instructions gave him a narrow window for this assignment, but that was not unusual.

These homes and grounds are designed for privacy, not security, which makes my job all the easier. This may be one of the most accommodating and luxurious neighborhoods I've ever bloodied up.

The man traveling as Schumacher took a deep, calming breath. A rush of cooler air brought by a breeze from the mountains reminded him of his primary home in Bavaria.

The Rockies are a poor second cousin to the Alps, but beautiful, nonetheless.

After responding to the personal ad to "Gunnar" in the **Sunday Times**, he had received instructions that included his target, her location, the required time frame, and pertinent personal information.

His designated victim is a middle-aged society woman with one grown child now living elsewhere. Fit enough, but not an athlete. No military or martial arts training. No weapons in the home. No guard dogs or pets. The alarm system is disabled due to a "service issue."

The home sits on a bluff top, a point of land

extending out from the rest of the homesites, over-looking a golf course fairway. No close neighbors. Tall hedges create a sound and sight barrier for anyone passing by. He has memorized his routes of escape, both the fastest and the most elusive, by car and on foot.

Mrs. Montgomery does appear to be alone in the home, as promised, which will make this a quick and clean operation, he thought as he walked through the garden gate left open for him. **Just business on this one. In and out.**

He moved up onto the front porch under an arched entrance and inserted the key provided to him in the oak front door, opening it and sliding in so swiftly that even someone standing directly in front of the house would not likely have seen him.

The front hallway is tiled in white marble. A large urn sits atop a black table in the center of the entrance hall. He had studied the layout of the house on documents left in his deposit box.

The kitchen is through that corridor on the right, located at the rear of the house. The lights are on. She is moving about, pouring a drink, a nightcap, perhaps.

He withdraws his loaded Smith & Wesson

revolver from his jacket pocket and then stands still again, tracking sounds in the kitchen and echoes throughout the mansion. The hum of appliances. The air conditioning kicking on. Ice clinking in a glass.

He steps away from the front door and moves into the corridor leading to the kitchen, crouched low, staying in the shadows as much as possible, scanning the floor with each step to make certain there are no obstacles in his path.

His target is facing the back windows of the house where faint moonlight is the only illumination. As he moves in on her, she senses his presence and turns with a gasp, her last dying breath. He presses the muzzle into her sternum and fires his first kill shot, resulting only in a light spray of blood.

He catches her body before she can fall to the floor and finds himself nose to nose with his target. Her eyes were wide with shock. He watched the light in them fade and then disappear into the final darkness. **Good night forever, Rich Bitch. I don't know your story, but I don't need to. You are a paycheck to me, an animal to slaughter.**

The killer eases Kathryn Montgomery's limp body to the floor. Her sturdy cocktail glass bounced but did not break on the imported hardwood floor. The remainder of her drink and several cubes of ice had spilled on him and then to the floor. He pays no attention. He is focused on finishing the job according to his contract. Six kill shots, no more, no less.

He presses the handgun muzzle into her lower abdomen and fires. He then targets both the right and left sides of her chest before flipping her body over and firing into the base of her spine. He flips her body over again and delivers a final shot with the muzzle pressed to her forehead.

Each shot is compressed against her flesh to muffle the sound. There are no exit wounds and no spent cartridges to worry about, exactly as planned. Blood from the six gaping wounds quickly pooled around the body, leaving stains on the knee of his jeans.

He stands over her, reveling in her death stare, which gives him pleasure. Not as much pleasure as watching a woman suffer at his hands, hearing her beg, but still, no little pleasure. The killer must fight the urge to take more time with her body.

No. They must find her body intact in her home for the client's purposes. This woman is not for my use. I will find another, later. In a more secure place.

He turns and leaves the kitchen, walking down the hallway to the front entrance. Bloody footprints leave a trail, which is not concerning to him. This is part of the client's plan. He opens the ornate oak door and quietly slips out onto the covered porch, locking the door behind him. From a dark corner there, he pauses for fifteen minutes, waiting to see if someone might have heard the shots and called the police.

All is quiet.

Sleep well, everyone. After this night, you may never sleep soundly again in those houses.

When he reaches his rental car, he pulls a gym bag from the back seat. He removes a box of baby wipes and cleans his face and hands. Then he removes his jacket, shirt, pants, and shoes, and puts on the shoes and clothing he'd stored in the bag. He will find an isolated place to burn the bloodied clothing before driving back to the airport in Denver.

As he drives out of The Spires Country Club community, the killer turns on the car radio and listens to the news.

"Colorado Springs police say they have no updates regarding the human hand found just off Gold Camp Road this afternoon. A police canine

search turned up no other body parts. Police say they have called off the canine search for now, but they will continue to investigate. Detective Joe Kenda told reporters earlier that identifying who the hand belonged to will prove difficult without additional evidence. He said anyone who has noticed suspicious activity along Gold Camp Road in the last week should contact police headquarters."

The killer found this report entertaining. He had scattered the prostitute's body parts in remote areas from Denver to Colorado Springs, knowing that predators would carry them even farther into the mountains.

Well, at least I was able to mix a little pleasure with my work on this trip. And tomorrow, the police will have a new case with a complete corpse rather than just a body part or two. I'm sure they will be grateful for that, though I doubt they would ever thank me for resisting the impulse to carve her into pieces. I would have enjoyed that so much more.

On his drive back to the airport and his "normal" life as German citizen Bruno Kleiss, the killer calmed himself by recalling other, more satisfying kills from his past. All of them women, many of them whores like his mother who had abused him so badly he'd been placed in a series of children's homes where the abuse escalated at the hands of other women, and men too.

THE MAKING OF A SOCIOPATH

Whether Bruno Kleiss was his real name was unknown even to him. Born in the outskirts of Brandenburg in 1945, he was taken by the state from his mother, a prostitute, at the age of seven. She'd been imprisoned for severely beating the boy. It wasn't the first time. On this occasion, his crime was wetting himself after she'd locked him in a bedroom closet while she was having sex with three men she'd solicited outside a bar.

From the ages of seven to fifteen, Bruno was confined to a Brandenburg home for "difficult children." Though described by officials as an orphanage, it was more of a prison camp. Bruno was one of thousands of children who became wards of East Germany's Communist dictatorship and lived in strict homes where they were indoctrinated to be better socialist persons.

Most of those children had done little more than

skip school or listen to forbidden music. Often, the government took them because their parents had protested the Communist regime or tried to escape to West Berlin.

Bruno's case was an exception, and so was his violent history. Like many of his fellow residents in the government home in Bad Freienwalde, Brandenburg, Bruno was sexually abused before and after his arrival there. His mother's boyfriends and lovers had raped him, and so did the staff members and security guards in the Brandenburg home. If he complained or fought them, they cut off his meals, put him in an isolation cell, or tortured him by shoving his head in toilets.

He was considered a delinquent, human filth, and unfit to live in the outside world. As he grew into his teen years, his tormentors began to consider him a threat. Bruno was smaller than most of those his age, but he was unusually strong and fast, a superior athlete. He was also street-smart, cunning, and cruel.

A loner, he preyed on his peers just as he'd been preyed upon throughout his life. The former Nazi soldiers who ran the juvenile home tried to break him, but with each beating and period of isolation, he grew stronger.

His secondary school teacher, Ilke Guilderland, a kind-hearted Danish woman just a year out of college, saw that, at sixteen, Bruno was an underachiever struggling with his studies. She offered to tutor him to raise his grades.

"You have abilities well beyond your performance in class, Bruno," she'd said. "Stay after class two days a week, and I will help you so that you can go on to Gymnasium for a better education when you leave here."

After their first tutoring session, Bruno followed her home, beat her, raped her, killed her, and mutilated her body. He then fled across the border into West Germany through an uncompleted section of the Berlin Wall, then being erected to stop the flow of East Germans leaving the repressive Communist state for the greater freedoms of the west.

To make the forbidden crossing, Bruno eluded land mines, booby traps, and the East German border guards, who were authorized to use deadly force to stop would-be escapees into West Berlin. He escaped by hiding inside a refrigerated meat truck after paying off the driver with money stolen from the teacher's home after he'd killed her, taken her keys, and searched her apartment.

When the border guards and their dogs inspected the inside of the truck's storage area, they saw only the bloody carcasses of freshly slaughtered cattle being taken to a processing center in West Berlin. Bruno had tunneled beneath the dead, frozen cattle to conceal himself and his scent.

From West Berlin, the teenager made his way three hundred miles to Munich by hitchhiking and hopping trains. He'd arrived in Munich only to be swept up in a police raid on an abandoned factory where more than one hundred homeless children, vagrants, prison escapees, and street gangs were encamped. Because he was still a minor, Bruno was placed in a boardinghouse run by the Sisters of Saint Mary Angela.

The Bavarian nuns matched Bruno's perversity and rage with their own. They rented out him and other children under their care as laborers for local farmers and, also, as easy prey for pedophile priests, businessmen, politicians, criminal gangs, and anyone else willing to pay. The nuns refused to allow any of their charges to be adopted or to move into foster care because their order had become dependent on the funds they collected from their abusers.

A few months after his seventeenth birthday,

Bruno rebelled when a nun, Sister Alberta, ordered him to report to the home of one of his most violent abusers. When he refused to go with the man, the nun drugged him and called the predator to pick him up. The boy was still unconscious when Herr Hoffman, a Munich arms dealer who had a horse farm outside the city, dragged him into his truck.

To awaken the boy, Herr Hoffman threw him into a filthy pond used by his horses and cattle. Bruno came to as the fat, naked German stood over him. Hoffman grabbed Bruno, but the slimy water covering the boy made him too slippery to get a grip. Bruno spun away from him.

"If you run, I will hunt you down with dogs that will rip you apart," Hoffman screamed as Bruno darted away, leapt a fence, and disappeared into the woods.

That night, the teenager returned to the Sisters of Saint Mary Angela boardinghouse and entered the nuns' quarters through an open window. He slashed the throat of Sister Alberta as she slept, gathered his clothing and few possessions in a gym bag, and fled.

Watching that bitch die was so sweet. I only wish I could have taken more time to make her suffer for all her sins. If she is a woman of God, I

want none of his church or his people. They hide behind their religion to inflict pain and suffering on those trusted to their care. I hate them all.

COVERING A BET

Fred Montgomery checked his Rolex as he was being escorted from the Whitehorse Casino on the Las Vegas Strip. The massive security beast on his right side, who appeared to be the world's largest Native American, jerked his arm back, but not before he could see that it was 10:00 p.m. back home in Colorado Springs.

The job should be done.

"You can let me go now, fellows. I am sorry for my actions, I must have had too much to drink," he said to his beefy escorts. "I won't be causing any more trouble."

"Too late, Mr. Montgomery," said the security escort, whose Whitehorse Casino name tag identified him as Lenny Blackbear. "I don't know what got into you tonight, but that kinda crap will get you banned from every joint in town. And I know you don't want that to happen."

"Okay, I get it, gentlemen," said Montgomery, who wasn't used to minions treating him roughly.

"Now, please, release me, and I will return to my suite for the rest of the night."

"Sorry, my friend, you will have to make your case with these **other** gentlemen who are waiting to escort you to a different sort of suite," growled the security guard as he and his coworker marched Montgomery out the front door.

Two Las Vegas Police Department patrol officers stood waiting with the back door of their squad car open.

"Wait, wait! I have never been arrested for anything! I know I was unruly this evening. I had a bad night. I will apologize personally to each and every person I offended, and I will make a large contribution to the charity of Mr. Bunyan's choice."

"Sorry, sir, but your whale status won't get you out of this one," said Blackbear, winking at the patrol officers.

"**Please, please!** I promise, I will even be a better tipper in the future," whined Montgomery.

The patrol officers handcuffed Montgomery and tucked him into the back of their squad car. They then huddled with the hulking security guards behind it.

"Thanks, guys. Mr. Bunyan doesn't want to press

charges on this rich prick because he loses a lot of money here," Blackbear said. "So have them lock him up for a couple hours and then release him so he can catch a flight and get his ass back to Colorado."

"Okay, Chief," said Patrol Sergeant Mark Spencer.

Blackbear glared at the cop, and then managed a smile that masked his malicious intent.

"Hey, you can call me Lenny, none of that chief shit! And if you want to come back when your shift ends, I'll buy you both some beers, and then I'll show you cowboys my tent full of squaws."

Three hours later, Fred Montgomery was released from the Clark County Jail with no charges filed. He took a cab to the Flamingo Hilton and went to his five-hundred-dollars-a-night luxury suite after being informed by the front desk manager that it was no longer being comped "due to a report on your conduct at the Whitehorse Casino this evening."

Well, at least there will be no doubt about where I was this weekend. I just hope my little act tonight doesn't get me banned from Vegas for good. Maybe my friend Morelli can fix things. He seems to be a man of many talents.

CHAPTER FIVE

COLD CALL

SUNDAY, JULY 13, 1975

Murder and mayhem, the evil spawn of a disorderly society, typically give it a rest on Sunday afternoons, but there are always exceptions. This Sunday started out calm and quiet, then revved up with a 2:00 p.m. call to our ever-vigilant 911 operators.

"I just returned from a weekend trip, and I guess I have a dead wife in my house," said the caller.

The cold words and matter-of-fact tone threw off the 911 operator. Thinking this might be a prankster, she asked the caller to repeat his statement.

"Like I said, I just got home, and my wife seems to be dead on the floor."

"Sir, what is your name and location, and how do you know she is dead?"

"Frederick Montgomery. Sixty-two hundred Aspen Lane in The Spires. And, well, the floor around her is just a mess. I don't know how I will ever get someone to clean up all this blood."

"Sir, I am sending a squad car and ambulance. Please go outside now, in case the killer is still in your home."

"Oh, I hadn't even thought of that."

MURDER IN A MANSION

The 911 dispatcher contacted Wilson. He called me.

"Coming to get you, Kenda. Get your butt out of the La-Z-Boy. We have a homicide up in the foothills in the fancy-pants neighborhood."

As I scrambled to my feet, I nearly spilled my beer and the entire snack tray Kathy had kindly prepared.

"I don't know why I ever try to watch any sports on television. The Grim Reaper just won't have it," I said.

"Only our Creator took Sunday off, kid," said Wilson, in a rare reference from his Bible Belt childhood. "Killers never rest."

I knew The Spires neighborhood for its

high-elevation location and matching home prices. The road to it crawls up the base of the Rampart Range of the Rocky Mountains outside the city proper, but that area was annexed a few years before I joined the force. Homes ran in the six-figures up there thanks to the large lots and panoramic views.

I checked a map. The house where the murder occurred was in a gated community at the end of a long, winding, and steep private road. It was a beautiful drive, and I dreaded every minute of it.

This is not something I talk much about, but I get carsick. It's been a problem all my life. No one would sit next to me in a car when I was growing up if the trip was farther than the grocery store. As a preventive measure, I popped a Dramamine just as Wilson pulled up to the curb in our unmarked Mercury Montego.

"How ya doing, Joe? Hope you didn't have a big lunch. We have some curvy roads, switchbacks, and hill-climbing ahead. I'm worried you'll puke in my hair! Ha!"

As the more senior homicide detective, Wilson was exercising his inalienable right to harass the shit out of his rookie partner. Cops are loyal to each other when faced with outside criticism or threats, but they are unbelievably vicious to each other when it comes to daily banter.

Rookies are always fair game. If the veteran cops spot a weakness, they go after it like predators picking off the weakest in a herd. **So, rookie, I hear you are afraid of the dark? Then you'll go first when we bash in the front door of the drug dealer's house at 3:00 a.m.**

Wilson's reference to me puking in his hair was another example of this rookie hazing. To my everlasting regret—and after far too many beers and shots of Irish whiskey—I had told him a few weeks earlier about my lifelong battle with carsickness.

Even worse, I'd handed him the fully loaded story of my first experience with it. I was only about five years old. My father took me along when he drove to pick up my mother at the beauty parlor. She had her hair done up all fancy for a party that night.

Mom danced out of the beauty parlor looking like a beauty queen. Dad gave her a wolf whistle and squeezed her leg when she sat beside him in the front seat.

"Wow, I am a lucky man!" Dad said.

Mom patted her new do.

"Sara did a very good job this time," she said, basking in the attention.

Dad put the car in gear, pulled out into traffic, and then made a sharp turn to head for home.

My stomach took its own bad turn.

There were no car seats back then, so I was untethered in the back seat. I'd stood up to give Mom a hug, and when the car swerved, so did my digestive tract.

I lurched forward and then projectile vomited all over Mom's freshly sculpted hair. Her screams of horror could be heard echoing in the deepest shafts of our Pennsylvania coal mines and across the highest elevations of the surrounding Appalachian, Allegheny, and Pocono mountains.

That day would live in family infamy. Why I shared the story of it with my relentless heckler in Homicide, I will never understand.

"Hey, Joe, how's the gut?" Wilson asked while cruelly pumping the gas and then the brakes and then the gas.

He only did it once, knowing that any more would bring Kenda contents gushing onto him.

"Still doing okay, buddy?" he taunted.

I gave him the finger and turned on the car radio.

Wilson countered by shoving a cassette into the tape player.

Loretta Lynn crooned on the car's lousy speakers, and I relaxed a little. I am a coal miner's son, after all. My only problem was Wilson growling backup harmonies. Loretta didn't need a stinking backup singer. I tried to shut him up by asking about our latest case.

"Hey, Wilson, have the crime scene guys come up with anything more on the hand dumped along Gold Camp Road last week?"

"Geez, Kenda, why do you have to bring up that pain in the ass case and ruin this brief peaceful interlude in our otherwise chaotic and blood-soaked lives?"

"Okay, so I guess that's a no."

The forty-five-minute drive took us up through most of Colorado's ecosystems, beginning with cottonwood willow and prairie grasslands and climbing to mountain shrubs, pinyon-juniper, and ponderosa pine. Once we cleared the gatehouse and approached 6200 Aspen Lane, the natural plant life gave way to artificially enhanced landscaping with over-the-top flowers, trees, and topiaries.

The five-acre lot turned crime scene offered

spectacular views of the Garden of the Gods and its red sandstone rock formations and, farther to the west, the region's most famous landmark, Pikes Peak, which was already dusted with snow at its highest point.

Patrol Officer James Jordan, who was first on the scene, stood in front of the house and, following procedure, gave us his somber assessment of the murder scene.

"Good afternoon, detectives. The deceased is female, fifty-nine years old, resident of this fine home. The victim's husband returned from a weekend trip, found her in the kitchen, dead from multiple gunshot wounds. You'll find the vic straight back at the end of that hallway. No signs of forcible entry. The husband said all doors were locked and secure. The alarm system was not functioning. He said it had been switched off for a while. We checked all side doors, back doors, and garage entry doors and all were secure. No indications of robbery or burglary as motive. Crime scene crew is on the way," he said.

"Thank you, kind sir," I said to Jordan. "Please make a note of anyone who shows up, including neighbors, the media, and police brass. Do not allow entry to anyone—including the brass—unless we authorize."

"Gotcha, Detective Kenda, and may I say, the new badge looks good on you, buddy."

Jordan and I had joined the force at the same time. He wouldn't be far behind me in moving up into the detective division. Jordan had a sharp mind and a keen eye for details. He grew up on the rough side of town, so he had some good sources in bad places.

"Hey, Joe, a couple more things," Jordan said. "The bereaved husband is a cold customer. No signs of grief. He's in his office, been on the phone the whole time, talking mostly about getting access to her bank accounts. The guy was inside when we arrived, so he was not concerned about the possibility of a killer still in the house. Once we escorted him outside, we searched all seven thousand square feet of the place and cleared it."

I thanked him, and we entered the home.

Kathryn Montgomery was our victim. I recognized the name as soon as the radio dispatcher identified her as the homeowner. Mrs. Montgomery was a noted philanthropist, civic cheerleader, and much beloved by local nonprofits and their fundraisers.

Her photo was featured in the local news almost

as much as mine would be later in my career. Mrs. Montgomery's coverage was mostly in the society pages. Mine wasn't. You may find that hard to believe, but it is true.

We found her body, as advertised, at the end of a hallway that led to the enormous kitchen. Even at first glance, Wilson and I had no doubt this was a homicide. No suicide has ever ended with so many close-range kill shots.

The late Mrs. Montgomery's eyes were open in a death stare, looking up from the blood-drenched kitchen floor. Wilson and I stood over her, looking but not touching as we made a preliminary assessment of the most obvious information to be gleaned before the coroner and crime scene team arrived.

"Smells like a good bourbon," I said, pointing to the cocktail glass on the floor.

"They all taste good to me," said Wilson.

There was a pressure contact gunshot wound to her forehead that left bone fragments in the blood-matted hair on the back of her head. A wound like that indicates that the shooter pressed the gun barrel into her forehead, compressing the flesh to the bone. When the killer pulled the trigger, the controlled explosion inside the weapon propelled the round at the speed of sound. The slug hit the skull, and the muzzle flash combined with burning powder, gas, and pressure to create an enormous entrance wound, leaving the skin around it blackened by third-degree burns.

This ring of scorched skin around a gunshot wound is called an abrasion collar. Any police officer, detective, or coroner recognizes this type of head wound as a sign that someone's brain has been turned into a puddle of soup.

"Our favorite coroner can tell us for sure when she gets here," Wilson said, "but I figure the shot to the forehead was most likely the final bullet fired, the coup de grâce. Some might call it overkill."

"I wouldn't argue that," I said, "though the shooter might."

We could not move the body to inspect her back—only the coroner could do that. There was more than enough damage to keep us busy examining the front of her body. Along with the head wound, there were four other massive bullet wounds visible; each shot was close range, and each left a gaping hole.

I could see one shot was to the center of the chest and through the heart.

Another chest wound was from a shot that appeared to be aimed at the spine and intended to sever the spinal cord.

A fourth wound was from a shot directed at her lung, which likely caused massive internal bleeding because the lungs are full of capillaries. Below that was a wound from a shot fired into the intestines. It would have resulted in waste spilling into the body cavity.

Just from the visible damage inflicted, we determined this was not a routine, spur-of-the-moment shooting. Each shot was calculated to inflict lethal damage. You'd think poor Mrs. Montgomery had flipped on a mob boss or stolen a ton of heroin from a Mexican cartel given the number of deadly rounds fired into her.

This appeared to be a professional hit, or a reasonable facsimile.

"Officer Jordan called it. Looks like we can rule out robbery as the motive," Wilson noted after a quick survey of the kitchen and the victim.

The victim was dressed in a designer blouse and slacks as if she'd just returned from a fancy dinner with friends. She wore enough diamonds to fund a cozy retirement in the South of France. One massive stone set in a ring appeared to be at least three carats in my nonexpert appraisal.

There was cash on the countertop above the body, a dozen hundred dollar bills paper-clipped together, and a list of names written on a Post-it note. This appeared to be the week's payments to the gardeners, lawn care crew, and household help.

Other than an empty cocktail glass on the floor nearby, there were no obvious signs of anything having been disturbed, moved, or taken from the scene. The massive kitchen, packed with high-dollar appliances, featured a stone fireplace and custom cabinets that might have been hand-carved for all the ornate flourishes.

"This place is right out of **Lifestyles of the Rich and Famous**," said Wilson, who watched too much television on his days off. "Hey, rook, what do you make of the shoe print and other imprints in the blood around the body?"

"Looks like our shooter knelt down to deliver the contact head shot," I said.

"Yeah, that's a cold move by someone who wasn't worried about being interrupted," Wilson said.

The crime scene techs came in lugging all their gear. Their supervising lieutenant, Marlin Bunting, nodded at us, then made a quick 360-degree survey before whistling softly.

"No muss, no fuss," he said. "The killer did a blow and go. A man on a mission."

Just then we were joined by "our favorite coroner," as Wilson had said, referring to our duly elected county official, the highly professional and well-respected Dr. Maggie Medina.

Maggie—I was allowed to use her first name only when we were both off-duty—was an exception on many levels among coroners in Colorado. The state requirements for the job were only that the coroner be eighteen or older, a US citizen, a resident of the county where he or she works, and have no felony convictions.

Given the low bar set by the state, the job tended to attract former undertakers, defrocked doctors, morgue ghouls, and political hacks. Dr. Medina was probably the most overqualified of any coroner in Colorado. She was an MD specializing in forensic pathology, and she had twice served as president of the American Society of Forensic Pathologists.

Wilson and I stepped back from the deceased, giving Dr. Medina room to work. She acknowledged us politely, but without a smile, given the setting. Nor did she pay any special attention to Wilson, which I found interesting since they'd been married more than ten years.

Wilson had told me they kept things professional in the workplace.

"We don't fraternize on the job, and we never talk shop at home," he told me when we first partnered up. "We don't even let our kids watch the news because we don't want them to see us being interviewed about any murders. It's bad enough that their parents share the same nightmares, we don't want the kids haunted by them too."

"Yeah, Kathy doesn't talk about her nursing patients, and I don't talk about what I see at work either," I said. "I wouldn't wish my nightmares on anyone."

Dr. Medina moved nimbly around the victim, making a quick inventory of the frontal wounds, and then she gently rolled Mrs. Montgomery's body onto its right side.

"The sixth bullet wound was a shot to her liver, another kill shot," she said. "You are not dealing with an amateur here, detectives."

"Yeah, we could not find any shell casings around the body, which is interesting," said Wilson. "What do you think, Joe?"

Wilson knew I was a serious gun guy.

"Either the killer used a revolver and the casings remained in the cylinder, or this shooter took the time to hunt down each of the casings and pick them up, which seems unlikely."

The coroner nodded.

"I'll be able to tell you more after the autopsy," she said. "For now, I'll just offer a preliminary finding that Mrs. Montgomery died of multiple gunshot wounds resulting in massive loss of blood. I'd put the time of death at early Saturday evening since she was still fully dressed."

"Okay," Wilson said. "We will leave you to your work. We have to talk to Mr. Montgomery in his office down the hall."

Fred Montgomery's home office was furnished like that of an Egyptian pharaoh. The gilded tables, chairs, and desks reminded me of photos I'd seen in promotions for the King Tut exhibit that was about to tour the country.

The newly widowed husband fit right in with the furniture, giving off the same gilded glow of wealth and privilege. He was once a dashing guy, no doubt, but his lifestyle had caught up to him—just over six feet, slight paunch, bloodshot eyes, and a "drinker's nose," as my grandmother would have described it.

"Mr. Montgomery, I'm Detective Wilson, and this is Detective Kenda. We are sorry to bother you at a time like this, but could we have a minute just for a few preliminary questions?" Wilson said.

Fred Montgomery glared at us like we'd tracked mud on his Egyptian Revival rug.

"Detectives, I will speak with you at some point, but right now I need time, and privacy, to call my daughter and inform her of her mother's passing," he said grimly.

"No problem," said Wilson. "We'd like you to come down to our headquarters tomorrow so we can talk about who might have killed your wife and whether she had any enemies who'd threatened her."

He gave a nod without looking up from his Rolodex.

"Sure," he said. "I'll bring my lawyer."

On our way out the large wooden front door, Wilson asked what I thought of Mr. Montgomery.

"Very stoic for a guy who just lost his wife," I said.

"Yeah, he's a cold one, no doubt about that," Wilson said. "But then, I've seen all kinds of emotions or lack of emotions from surviving spouses. You never know what is going on in their heads. He could just be in shock from the sudden loss. We'll give him the benefit of the doubt, for now."

This was a lesson Wilson offered many times in our early days together. The natural inclination in a case like this was to suspect the spouse first and foremost, but there was danger in that. You can fall into the trap of focusing too much on what may seem obvious and miss clues that point to other possible suspects worthy of attention.

In our business, jumping to conclusions can have serious repercussions.

As we walked to our car, Wilson surveyed the sprawling grounds with its meticulously groomed hedges, gardens, and grottos. Not a leaf on the ground. No weeds in sight.

"Like they say, young Detective Kenda, the rich are different, but that doesn't mean they are guilty. Or innocent."

CHAPTER SIX

LAWYERED UP

The rich are different in one way, certainly. They can hire better lawyers than most of the mopes we hauled in for questioning. Fred Montgomery's high-dollar mouthpiece showed up a half hour before his client to our scheduled interview at police headquarters. My guess was that the arrogant asshole came early so he had time to give me grief.

Harold "Hal" Jenkins, fifty-two, was the highest-paid criminal trial lawyer in the western United States. His jury presentations were better than anything found on television, the movies, or Broadway. He was tall, blue-eyed behind designer wire rims, and lean-bellied from his daily tennis matches. He paid more for his suits than I paid for my car.

Hal was an all-around smooth operator. Female clerks at the county courthouse called him "the Silver Fox" in reference to his sterling hair helmet and wily ways with the women. The county clerk had to schedule Hal's cases for the largest courtrooms to accommodate his lusty fan club along with the usual trial buffs and interested parties.

I wasn't one of Hal's admirers, though he had tried to screw me. When I was a patrolman, he stuck it to me on the witness stand. I'd busted a motorcycle gang member for doing ninety in a forty-five-mile-per-hour zone. Based on his glassy eyes and incoherent speech, I'd searched his Harley's saddlebags.

"Isn't it true you planted the cocaine that you claimed to find during your search?" Hal had said in front of the jury.

Luckily, the judge in this case wasn't one of Hal's tennis partners. He cut off the "unfounded line of questioning," knowing that the attorney was making a bullshit play to plant doubt about my truthfulness in the minds of the jurors.

I don't forget shit like that.

"Officer Kenda, it's been a while," Hal said as we waited for his client to show up.

"It's Detective Kenda now, Hal," I replied. "Are

you still driving the Mercedes 550 with the 'Slver-Fxx' license plates? Just checking in case one of our patrol officers spots you leaving the Colorado Club after a few cocktails. Again."

Hal had no comeback for that. He already had two DUI convictions. He couldn't afford another. Hal was known for telling his clients to rat out other criminals to win their own freedom. So the prisons were full of pissed-off thugs eager to shank him.

Wilson found our banter amusing, but off topic.

"Okay, buckaroos, enough with the friendly chit-chat," he said.

Fred Montgomery had entered the interview room without a word, but the scent of his failing deodorant and Glenfiddich breath told us all we needed to know. He was sweating through his custom-made suit jacket. His eyes were so painfully red I found myself blinking in sympathy.

He sat down hard and pulled his chair closer to Hal, whose $250-an-hour fee clock was already ticking.

"Mr. Montgomery, I'm sorry for your loss, sir," said Wilson. "I assure you that Detective Kenda and I will not rest until we find the person who murdered your wife and lock 'em up."

Montgomery offered no response. He stared at his folded hands on the table as if he expected them to answer for him.

Hal Jenkins had told his client to remain tight-lipped, which did not keep the whiskey vapors from betraying his morning nip. Someone had failed to gargle enough Listerine.

TREADING LIGHTLY

"Mr. Montgomery, do you know of anyone who might want to kill your wife?" said Wilson, keeping a close eye on Fred's body language.

His attorney tried to answer for him, but I waved him off.

"We'd like to hear it directly from your client, Mr. Jenkins," I said.

Montgomery seemed bored with the question. He scratched his chin with his index finger, sighed, and said, "Not a soul. Kathryn was beloved by everyone."

He was making no effort to help us, the dick, but Fred knew we would not put the screws to him, yet. Mr. Montgomery was not charged with a crime, and he had been informed of that. He was the husband of a murder victim and thus qualified as a victim himself, technically.

At this point, then, we were conducting an interview rather than an interrogation. Think of it as a first date. We were on good behavior. Not even pushing for a kiss on the cheek, let alone first base.

Your stalwart Detectives Wilson and Kenda were determined to be polite and patient even though we thought Fred reeked of guilt. In my early days, I tended to push too hard, prodding and poking and getting in my own way. Wilson had tried to teach me to tread lightly and politely in witness interviews.

"Even if the witness seems shady, you don't go in with guns blazing right out of the gate. You will only shoot yourself in the foot if you piss 'em off. This is especially true when there is a first-class trial lawyer like Jenkins in the room," he'd said.

An interrogation with a suspect, in contrast to an interview with a witness, is an effort to harvest damaging information from a target of the investigation. You are looking to trip up the subject who is lying to you.

Montgomery was still just a witness. We were not yet looking to poke any holes in his story. We were compiling information for an investigation that was gearing up.

The primary focus was answering a simple question: Who might benefit from the death of Kathryn

Montgomery? This murder was an intentional act done with a high level of cold-blooded expertise. What was the killer's motivation?

We presented ourselves as Montgomery's allies in the search for his wife's killer, not that he was buying it. As the victim's husband and likely heir to her fortune, Fred knew there was a target on his back.

Even so, Wilson did his best impression of a diplomat: "I'm sorry to bring you in here during this difficult time, but I have to ask a few questions, some of which might seem rude at this juncture. We have to ask them to help us focus the investigation."

"Go ahead, I'm listening," the husband said.

"How long have you known your wife?"

"Since college, so nearly forty years."

"How long have you been married to her?"

"We were married in 1938."

"Children?"

"A daughter, Samantha, born in 1940. She lives in Aspen with her husband and two children."

Fred Montgomery's attitude and body language were more important to us than whatever vague responses he mumbled. Several times, he looked up and away from us when answering, a potential sign that he was being evasive.

He also tended to tap both feet on the floor, releasing nervous energy, while keeping his eyes on the door, signaling a desire not to be helpful, but to get the hell out of the room.

Fred kept looking at his attorney before answering questions, which was not something you would expect him to do when we were only asking him about his relationship with his wife. He was acting more like a guarded suspect than a grieving spouse.

All of this was duly noted.

Wilson and I were the cats, and Mr. Montgomery was our ball of yarn. We gently pawed at him to gather as much information as possible while the case was fresh.

"Again, my apologies, but were there any recent marital difficulties?" Wilson inquired.

"No more than usual."

"Were there financial problems?"

"No, as you have seen, obviously we are very well off. Both of us."

"Well, you certainly have a beautiful home, but as you know, looks can be deceiving," I said.

(Couldn't resist, sorry, Wilson.)

"I assure you, Detective Kenda, my late wife and I have never lacked financial resources."

We were about to begin digging a little deeper into Fred's darker side, asking questions about things we'd learned in our preliminary investigation. We knew more than he thought we knew, but that's how the game is played. We had a long list of questions for Mr. Montgomery because we'd already churned up even more mud than we'd anticipated.

BEATING THE BUSHES

You can learn a great deal about a rich and arrogant asshole by talking to caddies, parking attendants, bartenders, and waitstaff at his hangouts.

Note to other high rollers: being cheap with the help doesn't pay.

Our first round of inquiries revealed that while most viewed Mrs. Montgomery as a candidate for sainthood, her husband was voted most likely to burn in hell.

"Some may pretend to like him, but most of us hope he'll end up dead in a ditch one day," offered a bartender at the club. "He cheats on the golf course, at the poker table, and in his marriage, which isn't that unusual for members here, but on top of all that, he's a lousy tipper and he welches on his gambling debts."

Nearly everyone we interviewed mentioned that Montgomery had a gambling addiction that ran the gamut from betting on the golf course to wagering on whatever was on television at the club's bar, whether it was professional bowling, horse races, or **The Dating Game.**

As a free-ranging lout, Fred bragged to friends about preying on rube poker players on gambling boats in Biloxi, Mississippi, and Peoria, Illinois, until he was banned for goosing a blackjack dealer in the former and thrown out of the latter for fondling a craps dealer who turned out to be the mayor's daughter.

Wilson and I had already put in for a trip to Las Vegas because we heard Fred had racked up debts with the mob and been banned from a couple casinos.

I'm sure Fred had some redeeming qualities. He had very white teeth, for example. Several people mentioned that Mrs. Montgomery had paid for all his dental work as well as his plastic surgery. Fred's face was pulled so tight that his eyebrows were permanently arched, making him appear perpetually surprised.

Fred married into his money, which might explain

why it flowed so easily through his fingers. His wife was the source of most of his wealth. Kathryn Cameron Montgomery was a Dallas heiress born into a deep well of Texas oil thanks to her great-grandfather Cam "Wildcat" Cameron. Somehow, the combination of her family's affluence, her years in Swiss boarding school, and membership in a Southern Methodist University sorority did not rot Kathryn's soul.

She defied the curse of fourth-generation entitlement. She didn't grow up as a spoiled brat, which is something of a miracle. Kathryn's only flaw was her taste in men. She met Fred when they were both studying at SMU. They locked eyes at a Greek formal party on the lush Dallas campus.

Fred was a junior on a swimming team scholarship with additional subsidies drawn from the abundant profits of Highland Park Sparkling Waters, his father's pool-cleaning empire.

Montgomery's father thought of himself as an entrepreneur, a self-made man. I'd give him that—if profiting from the labors of a vast army of low-paid immigrants fits that description. Maybe that's unfair. From our inquiries, we learned that a decent percentage of the Sparkling Waters pool-service employees were also drug abusers, work-release prisoners, and home-burglary scouts who cleaned the scuzz from the ponds and pools of the Dallas elite.

The owner's entitled son shunned the business, regarding pools as his path to athletic awards and sunbathing beauties drawn to over-chlorinated males. Kathryn was a sophomore majoring in fashion design when Fred's broad shoulders and cool arrogance caught her eye. She was even more impressed that Fred was studying to be a structural engineer and not a finance major like nearly every other SMU male.

"My Frederick is going to build things, not just make money off other people's money," she'd told her skeptical father.

EXPERT WITLESSNESS

Fred did not build any skyscrapers or bridges or even a single outhouse, despite his degree. In his first ten years after college, he was fired from a succession of engineering firms, mostly for his lack of interest in any actual engineering stuff. He spent most of his time placing bad bets and depleting his wife's pile of money.

For the first decade of their marriage, Kathryn held out hope that her husband would grow up one day. They had moved to Colorado to put distance between Fred and the revenge-minded Dallas bookies and loan sharks trying to claw back all that he owed them.

Once Kathryn had Fred tucked in her walled mountain retreat, she put him on an allowance and locked him out of her bank accounts. Fred's father already had cut him off from the family trust when he refused to join the pool-cleaning business, so Montgomery had to live off his spousal allowance until he hit a midlife jackpot.

When a shyster lawyer he'd met in a strip club learned Fred had an engineering degree, he enlisted him to serve as his expert witness in a civil lawsuit. The plaintiffs were parents of twenty-two kindergartners who were killed or injured when a bridge collapsed and crushed their school bus.

Fred's attorney friend was defending the company that built the bridge. They paid him a $40,000 fee, a.k.a. bribe, to testify that there was no problem with the bridge construction. Instead, he claimed "an act of God" in the form of a sinkhole had brought it down on the school bus.

After the defense dodged a $50 million bullet on that case, Fred was in big demand as an expert witness in similar lawsuits. He tapped a deep vein and joined a flourishing subculture that thrives in the complex world of criminal and civil litigation.

They are known as "expert witnesses" and while many of them were legit, Fred belonged to the "Hire a Liar" dirtbag subclass who would say whatever their shifty attorneys paid them to say.

Most expert witnesses make a good buck, paid by one side or the other in criminal or civil proceedings. Few of them are worth the money, in my opinion. A high percentage are so "expert," and so full of themselves, steeped in jargon and arcane science, that they either confound jurors or put them to sleep.

I had a homicide case in which the murder occurred in a freshly painted room. We arrested and charged a suspect based on a lot of evidence, including the fact that he had matching fresh paint all over his clothing and shoes.

To prove that it was the same paint, the prosecution called a chemist who was an expert in the composition of house paints. He was so god-awful on the stand with his charts and laser pointer and scientific babble that the prosecutor banned him from ever testifying in our county again.

"I could have painted my entire garage while he was on the stand," I told Wilson. "I think he's inhaled way too many fumes."

Though it is widely believed that the testimony of most expert witnesses is slanted to help the case of whoever is paying their fees, I have known a few who are honest and principled, including me. In my later years as a detective, the district attorney would often call me to testify about autopsies and how they were conducted because I had witnessed so many of them.

I can't say I enjoyed being an authority on how a forensic pathologist can turn a human body into a pile of garbage in a half hour. I don't like thinking about what happens on the autopsy table, let alone talking about it. There is one helpful thing about that expertise, however. I have found that bringing up this topic is a good way to clear unwanted guests out of the house: **Do you know that if you undergo an autopsy, your brain ends up in your stomach?**

It's bad enough that I have endless nightmares featuring the mutilated bodies that I've seen on the job. Attending autopsies and testifying about them in court only provoked more sleepless nights spent wrestling with the demonic visions that haunt most of us in law enforcement.

I wasn't even paid for my expert testimony on autopsies because I was already on the city payroll as a public servant. At least both sides knew I had no reason to lie about anything.

The only other truly honest expert witness I've known was my former neighbor Mike Curfee, who worked for the city's department of parks and recreation. Mike was an avid motorcycle guy. He and his father raced vintage motorcycles and won some major championships. Mike also taught motorcycle safety and driving classes for the local Harley Davidson dealership.

He was a stand-up guy, a good ol' country boy, who strolled around the neighborhood in his bare feet and charmed everyone with his friendly, humble ways. Many years after the Montgomery case, I ran into Mike while I was back visiting friends in Colorado Springs. We met later for a couple drinks, and he told me that the city attorney had asked him to serve as an expert witness in a civil case.

A motorcycle rider who'd crashed into a tree after drinking in a tavern was suing the city for $4 million, claiming the tree was planted too close to the road. The city attorney knew of Mike's motorcycle expertise and liked the fact that he could explain his views on the accident in his charming homespun way. He offered to pay him $150 an hour to provide his expertise on the case.

Hiring Mike proved to be a stroke of genius. Despite his "aw shucks" act, he has a PhD in motorcycles and a ton of street smarts. The hearings and depositions dragged on for more than a year, but, in the end, my friend made mincemeat of the lawsuit and the crash "victim."

"He was driving a Honda 1000RR, which is a lightweight 180-mph motorcycle, and this one was customized with all the go-fast bells and whistles, including a fancy exhaust and race tires," Mike told me. "But at a deposition, he claimed that he was driving the speed limit when he hit something that caused the bike to go down to the roadway, then a cable broke, which made it accelerate out of control and hit the tree."

Mike met with the city's lawyers after hearing that description of the accident and called bullshit.

"That's impossible because that particular motorcycle has a bank angle sensor that shuts off the motor when it tilts beyond a safe level," he told them, pulling out his laptop. "Here, I'll show you a demo video of how it works."

The normally stuffy lead lawyer nearly peed himself with excitement.

"You're fucking kidding me!" he said.

"They were so excited, you'd thought I'd just invented fire," my friend said.

But he wasn't done making his case against the biker's story.

"The judge let me examine his motorcycle helmet, and right away, I saw markings on it that showed he'd had a GoPro camera mounted on it," he said. "I recognized them because I had one on my own helmet, as do most motorcycle racers."

Mike told the city's lawyers to find out if the guy had a video recording of his accident. "You might check his social media because these street racers love to post videos of their crashes," he suggested.

The city's legal team filed a motion to get access to the guy's social media accounts. Sure enough, the dumb sumbitch had posted the videos right after the accident, along with this comment: "Oh man, I got drunk last night after breaking up with my girlfriend on my birthday and lost control of my bike at eighty miles an hour, crashed into a tree and really fucked up my body."

That put an end to the $4 million lawsuit against

the city, but his starring performance for the defense launched Mike on a lucrative second career as an expert witness in motorcycle-crash cases.

Good for him! I love it when honesty pays, and the good guys win.

Fred Montgomery, on the other hand, was neither honest nor good, according to all the dirt we'd dug up so far. His expert witness career lasted only a year or so before judges and lawyers figured out he was full of shit and had very little real-world engineering experience.

When that source of income dried up too, it made Fred even more desperate to get to his wife's money.

All of this made Fred an even likelier suspect. During our first talk with him, he certainly didn't give us any reason to give him a pass.

"Mr. Montgomery, when you arrived at your home on Sunday, how did you enter?"

"I had limousine service from the airport, so I entered through the front door with my key," he said.

"So, the front door was locked?"

"Yes, as I said. My wife was known for keeping the doors always locked. She was something of a fanatic about that."

"Mr. Montgomery, where were you in the days before you found your wife's body in your home last Sunday?" I asked.

"I was in Las Vegas on a business trip from Friday through that weekend with friends," he said. "I go there all the time."

And with that, Fred Montgomery offered up what would prove to be another poorly engineered project—his murder alibi.

"Thank you for your time, Mr. Montgomery. We will check out your story and get back to you," said Wilson. "Please don't leave the state of Colorado without notifying us. This is a priority case for us. We are working with the knowledge that your wife's killer is still out there. You should keep that in mind too."

CHAPTER SEVEN

ASPEN

I was nursing my first cup of coffee and organizing my notes on our Fred Montgomery interview when something metallic came flying out of nowhere, landed on my metal desktop with a loud **thunk!,** and scared the bejesus out of me.

"Sorry, rookie, did you shit yourself? Get our chariot gassed up, we're heading up to the rich hippy playground to talk with the Montgomerys' daughter," said Wilson. "While you're at it, wash the windshield and check the tires."

"Since when am I your personal valet?" I snarled.

"Since I wear the gold and you carry the silver, son," replied Wilson, flashing his corporal's badge.

I snatched up the wad of car keys he'd thrown on

my desk and cursed him all the way out the door and into the parking lot. His hooting laughter followed on my heels.

"Don't forget to pack your puke sack, Kenda!"

As my training officer, Wilson had seniority and the right to harass me, which he exercised gleefully, each and every day. I didn't like it, but I knew it could have been a lot worse.

Take what happened to Ross Verland, who was hired as a rookie patrol officer shortly after I joined the department. Verland made the mistake of telling his training officer that he had a fear of snakes. Wilson, the master prankster on the force, found out and made it his mission to terrorize Verland.

Unfortunately for the rookie, Wilson and his wife lived on a small place up in the foothills that we dubbed "Rattler Ranch" because it was crawling with rattlesnakes. Venomous vipers lurked under every rock and brush pile. Wilson was mean as a snake, so he fit right in.

One day, he showed up at headquarters with a bagful of snake, the biggest prairie rattler he could find on his land. The damn thing was six feet of coiled menace. Wilson killed it before bagging it, but Verland didn't know that. When he reported for duty on the late, late shift, he went to his squad car in the dark parking lot.

Wilson had removed the bulb from the patrol car's interior light, so the rookie didn't see the snake, posed on the driver's seat with its mouth gaping and fangs flashing.

When Verland sat on it, he came flying out of the car and emptied his gun into the snake's carcass. He then spotted Wilson laughing hysterically behind another car. The rookie reloaded and chased Wilson around the building threatening to blow him away too. The chief was not amused. He docked the pay of both Verland and Wilson and used the money to cover repairs to the bullet-riddled patrol car.

The chief also warned Wilson about taking hazing too far, so I had benefited from that. He had only subjected me to relentless verbal harassment.

"I'd let you take the wheel, but the state legislature just passed a law banning barfing and driving," Wilson said as we headed for the mountains.

Aspen was nearly a five-hour drive, so I didn't mind riding shotgun. The fur-swaddled resort town is only about 110 miles northwest of Colorado Springs as the crow flies, but, given the rugged terrain between the two cities, there was no fast and easy way to get there.

The shortest path was the 150-mile "scenic route" favored mostly by adventurous and often clueless tourists. It followed the Roaring Fork River on a twisting, steep, and narrow road notoriously lacking in guardrails. Flocks of wrecker trucks hovered along that route like vultures, waiting for cars to crash in the canyons.

Wilson knew better than to choose that rambling way, especially given my tendency to retch in transit. We set out on the safer, saner route that was mostly on the interstate highways (25 and 70), which took us up through Denver and then west through the Eisenhower Tunnel completed just two years earlier.

From there, we passed exits for many of Colorado's cowboy-chic resort destinations, including Breckenridge, Copper Mountain, Vail, Glenwood Springs, and Snowmass. This saner route added another 130 miles to the trip, but it wasn't an unpleasant drive given the scenery, especially if I took just enough Bonine to fend off carsickness without making me fall asleep.

If there is an ugly or boring view in the Rockies, I've yet to find it. Even so, the purpose of our trip through God's country dropped a dark veil over the drive.

"What do we know about the daughter, Samantha, and her relationship with her parents?" asked Wilson as he dodged Denver traffic on I-70.

I pulled out the notebook I'd packed for the trip, knowing Wilson would use the long haul to grill me on the case.

"From what I've dug up so far, the daughter seems to have hit the jackpot of life. She dodged Fred's genes, inheriting her mother's beauty, charm, and generous nature. She's also set up to get a sizable chunk of the family fortune—if her slimy skunk of a father doesn't blow it all on bad bets," I replied.

Samantha Montgomery Towers, the thirty-five-year-old daughter of Kathryn and Frederick Montgomery, had twins, Van and Sadie, after securing her PhD in English literature from Stanford University. She'd taught there for nearly ten years before marrying and starting a family of her own.

She wasn't just book smart. Samantha had proven to be much better than her mother when it came to choosing a spouse. Her husband, Trip, ten years her senior, had made his own fortune as a commodities trader adept at turning silos of Midwest grain into gold. Once he compiled enough cash to fill its own silo, he and his bride had moved to Aspen. There, Trip set about building an empire of high-end restaurants and bars catering to the rich hippy stoners who had overrun the former silver mining town in the early seventies.

"I can't stand Aspen," I told Wilson.

"What? Do you have something against snow bunnies wearing nothing under their parkas?"

"Snow bunnies, I can take, but I can't stand what comes with them. The town has become infested with fucked-up trust fund brats, celebrities in five-thousand-dollar ski suits, and coke-snorting faux cowboys in five-hundred-dollar Stetsons," I said. "It's been Californicated! Mostly thanks to that worthless train wreck of a **Rolling Stone** writer who ran for sheriff and lured all the twenty-year-old degenerates out of Malibu."

I was on a roll, or maybe a rant.

"We can't even trust the cops in that town. They drive Saab squad cars, for fuck's sake. They all wear long hair and smoke weed on the streets to seem cool. And on top of that, they do everything they can to screw with the DEA's undercover guys because they don't want them busting their dealers."

"Yeah, I didn't even bother to let the Aspen PD know we were coming to town. I didn't want to interrupt their white-powder orgies with the tourists," said Wilson.

He paused for a few minutes, and I could tell what was coming. My partner occasionally had flashbacks to his swinging single days as a musician on the road. He loved to tell those stories, and, for the most part, I didn't mind hearing them.

"Okay, I gotta admit, I did enjoy playing in Aspen back in my twenties when I was with my first Nashville band. After a gig one night, I walked into a bar and this beautiful older woman wrapped in a full-length mink coat walked up, gave me a lusty look, slipped her arm in mine, and walked me out the door. The next morning, I was sorely tempted to quit the band and spend the rest of my life in her bed. She wasn't a cougar. She was a saber-toothed tigress!"

We rolled into the rustic glitz of downtown Aspen as Wilson reminisced about his glory days. The only thing prettier than the scenery were the swells strolling on the sidewalks. Even the dogs trotting alongside them appeared to be best of breed.

"I always forget how beautiful this place is, but

it still makes my skin crawl," I said. "My wife and I came here a while back and I ordered a Coke in a bar; it cost eight dollars! Kathy said this town explains why the peasants want to kill the rich people."

Wilson drove through town and into the outskirts where the homes were hidden behind rock formations or heavy gates. Samantha and Trip Towers lived in a mansion they'd bought a couple years earlier after its previous owner, a race-car-driving heir to the Woolworth fortune, died in a small plane crash just outside of town.

Planes crashed with unsettling frequency when flying in and out of Aspen, averaging nearly one a year. Maybe it was the thin air, or the fact that the Aspen airport, ranked the most dangerous in the United States, had one runway with mountains at each end. I'd heard pilots say that landing there was like dropping out of the sky into a wind tunnel.

Wilson pulled up to the gate at the Towers' home, about two miles south of downtown, off State Road 82. Ten acres of mountain streams, ponds, wildflower gardens, stone terraces, and natural rock formations with mind-blowing views of Independence Pass and Aspen Mountain. When Samantha Towers opened the huge wooden front door, I was briefly blinded by the sun streaming through the floor-to-ceiling windows.

I'd thought her parents lived in the fanciest home I'd ever seen, but Samantha's place was bigger, warmer, and, well, spectacular, like a massive Yellowstone lodge but with a much higher decorating budget. The river rock fireplace in the great room was three stories high. Antlers, Indian blankets, Old West photographs and paintings, peace pipes, headdresses, and other artifacts hung from the walls. Every piece of furniture was covered in leather that smelled of money.

"Detectives, please come in," said the daughter of our victim, her voice shaking. The red rims of her teary eyes let us know she was still deep in mourning.

My awe of our surroundings gave way to sympathy for the lady of the house. No amount of money or material goods can ease the grief she was experiencing.

"Would you like some coffee?"

"Yes, please, that would be great," said Wilson, laying on the Nashville drawl.

She was a striking woman, with her mother's emerald-green eyes, but with soft, curling long black hair. She wore a flowing dress in a Navajo pattern that looked like it, too, could be hung on the wall.

She pointed to the library and den off the great room. We headed that way. When Samantha returned with our coffee cups on a silver tray, she caught Wilson picking up an old black cowboy hat from a tabletop.

"That once belonged to John Wayne, but I can't remember what movie he wore it in," she said.

Wilson, who worshipped "the Duke," froze at her words, then reverently returned his hero's hat to the desk, bowing over it like an altar boy over a sacred chalice.

We sat with the daughter at a small table in a corner of the library, surrounded by four walls of books. A quick glance revealed that most were about the Rockies, the Old West, and the history of Aspen in the years prior to the invasion of Hunter S. Thompson and his zombie cowboy cult.

"Mrs. Towers, we are sorry to intrude on your grieving, but we are here to ask for your assistance in our investigation and search for whoever killed your mother," said Wilson, still in a reverential mode.

"I understand, Detective Wilson, although I don't think I can be of much help," she said. "I can't imagine anyone wanting to harm my mother in any way, let alone in this gruesome manner."

Apparently, Fred Montgomery had not spared his daughter the gory details in describing his wife's murder. Another indication that he is a cold bastard, but it did spare us from having to break that awful news to her.

"I guess our main interest today, is just what you mentioned, trying to determine if there was anyone who might have wanted to hurt your mother because this did not appear to be a random act or a burglary that she interrupted," Wilson said.

"You know as well as I do that my mother was renowned for her grace and generosity," said Samantha Towers. "Like I said . . ."

Wilson plunged ahead, getting impatient with the niceties, apparently.

"What about her relationship with your father? Were they on good terms?"

Mrs. Towers's tone turned cold.

"I'm not sure what you are asking me?"

"It's just a question we have to ask, I'm sorry if I offended you," said Wilson, scrambling to keep the interview from going sour.

"Is everything okay, Sammie?" said Trip Towers, stepping into the room.

Hollywood hair. Blue denim shirt. Old jeans.

Perfectly aged ostrich-leather cowboy boots. He looked like a young Clint Eastwood on the set of **Rawhide**, sizing up a couple of cattle rustlers caught red-handed with a bawling calf.

"I'm fine, just trying to help the detectives with their investigation," his wife said.

Her tone was calm. Her eyes said, "Help me!"

Trip walked over to his wife and gently massaged her shoulders. Wilson and I pretended to study the bookcases for our favorite romance novels.

"Just wanted to let you know the kids and I are back," Trip said gently. "I'm making them lunch. Can I offer any of you a snack or sandwich?"

"No, we're fine, but thank you," said Wilson.

Personally, I could have used a bratwurst and beer, but I kept my mouth shut. We had more questions to ask.

Trip shot us one more "don't fuck with my wife" warning glare and walked out. He seemed like a class act. If it had been my wife sitting with two homicide detectives, I might have pulled up a chair and become an overly protective pain in the ass.

Wilson went back to work. "Mrs. Towers, let me ask you this: Is there anyone who stands to gain—in any way—from the death of your mother? I mean, maybe this wasn't personal. Maybe it was about removing her to get access to something, whether it be money, power, social standing, or any other form of personal gain."

It was a good question because Kathryn Montgomery had all those things—money, power, and social standing. Given the highly competitive ways of those in the upper crust, maybe an overzealous society matron had knocked off Mrs. Montgomery so she could claim her seat on the board of some charity.

"I understand what you are asking, Detective Wilson, but I really would have to give more thought to that because my mother was involved in so many organizations, from nonprofits to corporate boards, private schools and soup kitchens," she said. "You know her reputation as well as I do; she was not known for making enemies. She was known for making a positive difference wherever she went."

Wilson played another card.

"Was money ever an issue between your parents?"

I half expected Samantha Towers to toss her coffee at Wilson's face, but she was raised by a strong woman and had obviously learned from her example. Anger flashed in her eyes for an instant, then resolve.

"I love my father. She loved him too. It's no secret that my mother came from a wealthier background and that my father never had the success as an engineer that he'd hoped for," she said carefully. "Even so, he seemed to earn quite substantial sums as an expert witness, and I never knew money to be an issue for either of them."

"Or between them?" Wilson asked.

"Detectives, as you can see, my husband and I live quite comfortably, but even we have had our battles over finances. I doubt that there is a couple outside of England's royal family that hasn't had conflicts over money matters," she said.

"Mrs. Towers, respectfully, we aren't local reporters here to uncover family secrets. We are homicide detectives trying to track down a killer who brutally—and expertly—executed your mother in a manner that points to a highly trained professional," Wilson said. "This appears to have been a calculated killing. There seems to be nothing random about it. So, we need you to help us find the person who murdered your mother so that we can bring him—or her—to justice, while making sure no other family suffers as you have.

"That said," Wilson added, "we are aware that

your father had a gambling problem and had incurred serious debts over the years, so I repeat, was money ever an issue between your parents?"

Samantha Towers did not break or bend, but she found a way to answer without betraying the trust of either parent.

"Detective Wilson, honestly, I did my best to stay out of my parents' financial affairs and I always made it clear to them that I did not want to take sides in their relationship," she said. "For that reason, neither of them confided in me. But my mother did confide in the two men who have served as her financial advisors ever since she became an adult. I am executor of her estate and I have power of attorney over it now, so, if I provide you with their contact information and tell them they have my permission to cooperate in your investigation, can we please call it a day?"

"Okay, we'll talk to them, but we may have to come back to you if we have more questions," I said. "We are doing our best to see that your mother's killer is brought to justice."

"Yes, I understand. Thank you, detectives," she said.

On the way to our car, a thought came to me,

the answer to a question that had been churning in my brain.

"**The Searchers**," I said to Wilson.

"What the hell are you talking about, Kenda?"

"**The Searchers**. John Wayne wore that black cowboy hat in that movie," I said. "Nineteen fifty-six. John Ford directed. Great film. A classic!"

Wilson crammed his lanky frame into the driver's seat before acknowledging my astounding depth of knowledge about one of his favorite topics.

"Well damn, rookie, you are just full of fucking surprises. Now pop another pill so you don't spew them all over the car on the way home."

CHAPTER EIGHT

THE AUTOPSY

My first rotten corpse was nineteen years old, prior to being nine days dead. I was still a patrolman and not at all prepared to deal with a body that had been baking that long in an airless apartment during a July heatwave.

Love ended in death for this victim. Her boyfriend had promised to marry her, but instead, he dumped her for another girl. She cried and screamed and brooded about it for weeks. Then, she put a 9mm handgun in her mouth and pulled the trigger.

We were dispatched to her apartment nine days later when other residents complained of an awful odor. The apartment was not air-conditioned, which sped up the timetable for decomposition, magnifying the horror of the scene.

The smell hit me as we were walking up the stairs to her apartment. I staggered back.

"Rookie pussy," muttered my patrol partner back then, Rick Baker, laughing scornfully.

How can you laugh? I wondered.

Then Baker opened the door, unleashing an oven-baked stench that sent me reeling and nearly falling into the maggot-infested remains of what had been a pretty, young Hispanic girl.

I went back outside and threw up in the hallway, triggering more scorn from my veteran partner. I could not get that vision out of my head or the putrid reek out of my nostrils for years. Both still haunt my dreams. Rotting corpses were prominent in my first series of unrelenting nightmares. They often began in this young woman's apartment.

Check the back of her head for an exit wound, we need to know if the bullet passed through her skull and went through the wall somewhere, Baker says.

I pick up what only slightly resembles a human head, and it crumbles into oozing pieces.

Usually, this is where I wake up, either on my own, or after being belted by Kathy because I've been screaming and groaning in my sleep. I never tell her what I've seen, in the dream or on the job. I don't want to burden her or the kids with my nightmares, so I keep them to myself.

That proved to be a mistake that compounded my misery over many years. There were professionals available even back then, but I didn't want to appear weak. I didn't want a visit to the department's psychologist on my record.

Autopsies always triggered my worst nights. The terrifying visions come fast and furious whether it is the night before or the night after. For the first years, the autopsies themselves were as bad or worse. Over time, I learned to disassociate from the experience itself. But not the haunted dreams, they have never ended.

A FRUITFUL EXAMINATION

Most autopsies are grim, disturbing, and dehumanizing. Wilson is the only guy I know who had a funny story about one, though, it is definitely "dark humor" of the sort that cops, coroners, and first responders brandish to fend off the demons. Here's Wilson's story. I'm retelling it from memory because I had to listen to it at least once a month during my rookie days:

Wilson and his former partner were dispatched

to a low-end apartment complex after the manager found one of his residents dead. His coworkers had come to check on the guy when he failed to show up for his janitor job. When the manager opened the door, Wilson knew right away that the occupant was into some kinky shit. Porn magazines and photographs littered the floors and tabletops, along with empty bottles of cheap wine and bad whiskey.

The magazines and photographs were of the S&M genre, a subculture for perverts into pain. Cops run into S&M creeps often because they tend to meet with the Grim Reaper prematurely due to their dangerous sex games, which often involve choke collars, whips, vices, and leather bodysuits.

Wilson entered the bedroom of the apartment and found the AWOL janitor dead on the floor in a pile of more porn and booze bottles. There was a leather choke chain around his neck. The leather strap connected to the choke chain was tied to his bedpost. The strap was pulled taut, indicating that the janitor, while in the throes of a drunken S&M act, had passed out, fallen off the bed, and strangled himself.

This happens more often than you might think. The official name for this is "autoerotic asphyxia" or "death by sexual misadventure." Usually self-inflicted, it is rarely mentioned in the newspaper obituaries of the deceased.

In this case, the janitor added his own special twists. The guy was wearing an entire leather ensemble—bra, girdle, and high heels. He had wooden clothes pins fastened to his balls.

It gets worse.

Wilson went to the autopsy just in case the coroner found evidence that someone else might have been involved in the janitor's twisted death. The coroner back then was the ancient Dr. Hans Gschwendtner. While he was examining the anal cavity of the deceased, the German-born physician suddenly stopped, looked up at Wilson, and said, "Vot haff ve here?"

He then put a set of forceps into that cavity and pulled out first one medium-sized orange and then another.

"Oranges?" Wilson said.

"Vell, Detective Vilson," said the coroner. "All I can tell you is, they aren't tangerines!"

Like I said, Wilson loved to tell that story, but I noticed that whenever we had breakfast together, he skipped the orange juice.

NOT A TRACE

Dr. Maggie Medina succeeded Dr. Gschwendtner after he retired. A tiny woman with a formidable intellect, she raised the bar in her profession, though she had to stand on a bench to view all the havoc six close-range gunshots wreaked upon the body of Mrs. Kathryn Montgomery.

"Do you want me to hold the light bar for you?" Wilson asked.

"No, stay back, please. I have done this many times. Besides, I don't want anything splattering on you that I have to explain to the dry cleaner later," she told her husband.

I had stepped up to offer my services, only to back off when Dr. Medina waved her scalpel at me. I learned long ago not to mess with small women brandishing sharp blades. The coroner returned to dictating her observations during the exam into a microphone hanging from the ceiling, so I was content to stay a couple steps back, threat or no threat.

I never could stomach autopsies, even after I'd witnessed hundreds of them. Carnage was part of my job, but if I didn't need to see it, I preferred not to add to the gory images already in my file of horrors. I had also learned to block out the smells of the autopsy room in the same way I kept them at bay at crime scenes with overripe corpses. One of Dr. Medina's assistants had helped me deal with the foul odors. The assistant, Maddie, saw me struggling during an autopsy and pulled me aside.

"Here, use this, it works like magic," she said, placing a small blue jar with a spin lid in my hand.

I looked down. It was a jar of Vicks VapoRub, the same smelly gunk my mother used to rub on our chests when we had colds as kids.

"Just rub a little bit under your nose, or put it on a handkerchief to hold under your nose," Maddie said. "The menthol blocks out other odors and clears your pipes all at the same time. You'll learn to love it."

She was right, and from that point on, I never left for work without a small jar of VapoRub in my pocket. I even came to find the menthol smell soothing when standing in the chaos of a crime scene, or in the sterile stench of a morgue.

Dr. Medina's cool professionalism was another calming influence in that environment. Professional competence always has that effect on me, and this lady knew what she was doing. We were counting on her help in this case more than most. Mrs. Montgomery had died from six expertly administered, close-range rounds and the massive damage they inflicted. Despite all the ammo fired into her body, we had collected no bullet casings or fragments at the scene. This was highly unusual.

"It's really bugging me that we couldn't find anything when we were there yesterday," Wilson had said on our drive to the county morgue.

Dr. Medina realized how important it was for us to get a handle on the unusual method used in this murder. Identifying the weapon and the type of bullets usually brought us a step closer to identifying a suspect.

We were not overrun with helpful evidence at this point. Mrs. Montgomery's sketchy husband, Frederick, had an alibi, which we were examining with a microscope. He had motive, but did he have the wherewithal? The placement of the shots and lack of evidence at the crime scene indicated a high level of calculation and expertise. Mr. Montgomery was an engineer, though not a very good one, and we hadn't found anything indicating he owned a gun, or that he had weapons training.

We were hurting for direction with this investigation and the pressure was on. We'd held off the media hounds so far, but there was no doubt they'd eventually be barking and yowling at the gate. Mrs. Montgomery was high profile in life and in death. Her social standing and popularity throughout the region made this a case of great interest to the public in general, as well as to power brokers and political leaders who were not shy about calling the police chief for daily updates.

There was another pressing concern: if this killer was on the run, he or she might strike again while we were chasing shadows. That sort of thing could put a damper on a detective's career. This all weighed heavily upon those of us in the room.

"Hand me that metal probe, Detective Kenda," said the medical examiner. "I will now search for bullet fragments inside the body."

The entry wounds were larger than any I'd seen. It would follow, then, that there would be many fragments. Dr. Medina probed for more than an hour, searching along the path of each of the six bullets, without finding any remnants.

"I don't mind telling you that this is a bit bewildering," she said. "I have traced every one of the paths. There are no exit wounds, and no fragments that I can detect."

Most handgun ammunition is cased in a copper

jacket. When the bullet is fired into a body, that thin layer of copper splits away and leaves fragments along its path. If the killer used hollow-point bullets, which would explode inside the body and make no exit wound, there still would be some traces of copper detectable.

After Dr. Medina probed all six wounds and found no metal remnants, she opened the corpse to examine the organs, making a Y-shaped incision, and removed the breast plate with giant bolt cutters.

She examined the exposed organs nearest each wound, searching for fragments.

"There are no exit wounds and no fragments detectable in the body," she said. "It's as if the bullets disintegrated upon impact."

Dr. Medina climbed down from the stool to take a break. Wilson and I walked a few feet away to give her room.

"What sort of ammunition disintegrates without a trace?" Wilson asked.

"I have never seen anything like this," his wife said.

My brain was running through all the different types of ammunition I'd used as a patrolman and detective. None of it disintegrated completely on impact. Then, I thought about the ammo I used in shooting competitions and target practice outside of work. A thought hit me.

"What about wadcutters?"

Those words came blurting out of my mouth so quickly I surprised myself.

"What the hell are wadcutters?" Dr. Medina asked. "What are you talking about, Joe?"

"We use them when shooting at paper targets because they leave a perfect hole," I said. "They are made of soft lead, like a plumber's lead, used to solder and repair metal pipes. Wadcutters don't have a rounded nose like most bullets. They are flat on both ends, slightly concave, and designed to punch holes in the target paper."

Dr. Medina mulled this over.

"I've never heard of that sort of ammo being used in a shooting. Could these whatever-cutters do this much damage to a body?" Wilson asked. "And what sort of gun would you use? Not a target pistol, right?"

"The killer was right on top of her. Every shot was close range, so yes, that kind of soft-lead ammunition would create these large entry wounds and then cause massive damage like this while disintegrating in the body without leaving a trace."

I'd never heard of it being used to shoot a person, but it would eliminate any chance of using fragments as evidence.

"The murder weapon had to be a revolver because a flat-nosed round like these will not chamber in a semi-automatic pistol," I said. "This killer didn't want to leave any trace for us to follow. We aren't looking for some idiot kid who surprised Mrs. Montgomery during a burglary. This guy, if it was a guy, knew his firearms. He left no tracks or traces for us to work with."

The three of us looked with a new perspective at the devastated body on the autopsy table, wondering why anyone would take such calculated measures to kill this admirable and generous woman.

"Joe, I will need your help figuring out how to write up a query to other law enforcement agencies asking if they've ever run across a shooting with this type of ammo," Wilson said. "What's it called again?"

"Wadcutters," I said.

"Wadcutters?" Dr. Maggie repeated.

Wilson couldn't help but smile.

"Congratulations, Joe. You just taught something new to a woman with six years of medical training, five years as a coroner, and an IQ that is off the charts."

CHAPTER NINE

ALL ABOUT THE MONEY

A week into the investigation of Kathryn Montgomery's murder, we had nada.

This respected community leader had no enemies that we'd uncovered. We'd found no skeletons in her closet. She had no addictions or vices that might have made her a target.

The crime scene crew came up with nothing useful, as we had feared. The shoe print found in the victim's blood was from a size ten and a half, D-width Nike athletic shoe, a size and a brand worn by hundreds of millions of people. The knee print left in the blood on the floor when the killer knelt beside her was from a pair of Levi's 501 jeans, also worn by millions upon millions.

Wilson claimed he had a couple dozen pairs in his own closet.

Fred said the security system had been malfunctioning, but they hadn't gotten around to having it serviced. He had no real explanation for the open back gate other than blaming the gardener or lawn service. The fact that the killer entered and left even though all the doors to the house were locked raised a lot of questions, but we had no answers.

Montgomery could have been lying about the front door being locked when he returned home on Sunday, of course. Lying seemed to come naturally to him.

"Both her husband and her daughter said Mrs. Montgomery was very conscientious about keeping the doors locked all the time. Samantha told us her mother was known for locking them out of the house even if they'd just gone out to get the mail," I said.

"And the crime scene unit said they had a locksmith take apart and examine all the locks on the exterior doors in the house. He found no signs that any of them had been picked," said Wilson.

"I suppose she could have forgotten just one time

to lock a door, but that seems unlikely given what we know about her," he added. "The front and back door locks are expensive brands that can only be locked and unlocked with a key, so if someone got in, they had to have one."

"Yeah, and, again, both Fred and the daughter said that there was no key stashed outside under a welcome mat or a garden rock. They were more security conscious than most families, it seemed," I said. "I guess having a bajillion dollars will do that to you."

Then Wilson noted something I'd been thinking too.

"As fucked up as it might sound, the best thing we have is the fact that Fred Montgomery's alibi is suspiciously tight and tidy," he said. "A cynical detective might look at it and think that Fred took special pains to let the world know that he was in Las Vegas on the weekend his wife was plugged six times in our jurisdiction."

I'd had a call with Detective Doug Birch of the Las Vegas PD. We were buddies, sort of. I'd once done him a favor in a Vegas case that leaked over into Colorado Springs, so I'd asked him to do some checking on Montgomery's activities that weekend.

Birch was head of Vice in the vice capital of the country. A slightly reformed gambler who confined himself to the slot machines, Detective Birch knew all the players at all levels in Vegas. Even better, his big brother, Lenny, was an undercover agent planted by the feds on the security staff at the Whitehorse Casino, which was crawling with mobsters and the dirtiest of dirtbags.

"Brother Lenny says Montgomery is a regular on the Strip and at their place where he gets everything comped only because he tends to lose a lot more than he wins," said Detective Birch. "He has never been on security's radar in the past, but on this occasion, he seemed to be trying his best to put on a public display of assheadedness.

"Lenny had to have him hauled out of the joint and arrested after raising a ruckus," the Vegas detective added. "He grabbed the ass of one of our waitresses and then cussed out a pit boss. Lenny's boss dropped the charges, but Fred won't get any free drinks or buffets for a while."

Wilson thought the Whitehorse incident sounded like a stunt too.

"Fred is a calculating and controlling asshole, so I'm not buying that he just had a bad night in

Vegas," my partner said. "Looks to me like he was establishing his alibi. But good luck on convincing a jury of that. He may have hired someone to do his dirty work while he was out of town, but we have a tough row to hoe proving that was the case."

I'd been thinking about that and wondering if Montgomery's previous trips to Vegas weren't just for gambling.

"Maybe we need to know more about Fred's Vegas connections, if you get what I mean," I said to Wilson. "I'll ask Detective Birch to have his brother do more digging. We can put him on our Christmas list if he comes through."

MOTIVE ISN'T ENOUGH

Fred Montgomery was number one with a bullet on our suspect list, but as Wilson said, "Other than the fact that he is a renowned asshole and a bad gambler, we have diddly squat when it comes to connecting him to his wife's murder."

We needed to know who murdered Kathryn Montgomery before we could find out whether the killer was connected to Fred. Usually, we aren't all that concerned about motive in a case. Motive is overrated, thanks to thespians posing as detectives.

Motive doesn't get convictions. We concentrate on evidence, but until we found some in this case, motive was about all we had to look at.

The usual triggers for a murder are fear, rage, revenge, lust, money, and, last but not least, sheer madness. It was way too early to rule out any one of them, or any combination of them, but we kept coming back to money as the most likely trigger in this case.

"If the motive is money, Fred would seem to have the most skin in that game," said Wilson. "She had cut him off from her finances but kept him in the will as her main beneficiary—and her estate is worth a bundle from what we've heard."

Kathryn was from serious Texas oil wealth that went back a couple generations. That made it "old money" by Texas standards, though in most European countries, they'd been considered nouveau riche.

Fred's father was loaded thanks to the pool-cleaning empire he'd built, but his son preferred sunbathing to pool cleaning, so Dad cut him off after college. Fred wasn't much of an engineer either. He had managed to find a lucrative niche as an expert witness in civil trials. Still, that income was sporadic and, while sometimes substantial, not enough to keep him afloat given his gambling habits.

Fred's losses were steep from what we were hearing. Our own Vice division and our friend working undercover on the Whitehorse security team reported that Fred had been banned from the private high-stakes poker games that were staged secretly in mansions and private clubs around Colorado, and in Vegas too.

We'd also heard country club gossip that Fred had complained to golf buddies about Kathryn keeping him on a tight leash even though "the bitch gets richer every fucking day."

Based on that information and the advice of the victim's daughter, Samantha, we scheduled a meeting with Kathryn's financial advisors at Donaldo & Oskowitz Wealth Management. The names on the door were not thrilled that we wanted to talk to them. They tried to stonewall us at first, citing a smorgasbord of confidentiality and client privilege mumbo jumbo.

"We have frozen Mrs. Montgomery's accounts, as required by law, and we are waiting to hear from her attorney or executor," said Donaldo, giving us the stiff arm.

"Samantha Montgomery Tower is the executor of her estate, and she has power of attorney, as I'm sure she told you when she called and instructed you to cooperate with us," said Wilson.

Donaldo hemmed.

Oskowitz hawed.

"Well, that may be the case, but due to federal and state privacy laws regarding client financial information, we will need to consult with our attorneys and our corporate headquarters before sharing any of Mrs. Montgomery's information with you gentlemen," said Donaldo while shuffling papers on his antique desk.

This was not my savvy partner's first line dance with high-dollar stonewallers.

"Well, fellers, I guess we can always call our friendly neighborhood judge and get a subpoena to comb through **all** your records, given the severity of this case, but, in my experience, I'm just warning you, that once we start digging into your files we are legally bound to report any questionable materials we come across, for example, any evidence that you have set up illegal offshore accounts, or any hint of inappropriate billing practices. I'm sure our friends with the IRS and the feds would be interested in that sort of information," said Wilson, unleashing his best cowboy **Columbo** bullshit.

Wilson had them at "illegal offshore accounts."

"Okay, gentlemen, we get the point," said Donaldo as he loosened the knot on his tie. "In recent years, Kathryn had become more and more concerned about her husband's gambling addiction. She told us a few months ago that he seemed to be getting desperate. She had given him hundreds of thousands of dollars to pay his gambling debts, and still he wanted more."

Donaldo wasn't used to sharing client information and he was sweating profusely. I worried that he might have a heart attack.

Seeing the same signs of anxiety, Oskowitz stepped up and took the baton. "She had discovered earlier this year that her husband had been stealing checks and forging her signature on them to cover new gambling debts. He also had sold the rare sports car she'd given him as a wedding present. She assumed that was also to pay off his debts."

"Just out of curiosity, what kind of car was it?" I asked, being a car guy myself.

"A 1938 Bugatti Type 57S Atalante Coupe," said Oskowitz. "I believe he sold it to another collector for around two hundred fifty thousand dollars."

I would have been more impressed if I had any idea what a Bugatti looked like. I was more of a Mustang guy.

"So, did you do anything to protect her dough from the asshole," said Wilson, who enjoyed cutting to the chase.

"She had asked us to look into creating a spendthrift trust, which we had advised her to do for many years, given her husband's profligate ways," said Donaldo, whose heart rate must have settled down.

"'Profligate?' That's a very fancy-ass way of putting it," said Wilson.

"What exactly is a spendthrift trust?" I asked.

The bean counters smiled. They loved schooling the poor proletariat on the ways of the moneyed class.

"Well, let's just say a client has a spouse who is not financially independent and not capable of managing finances—and, perhaps, tends to incur debt that might endanger the client's holdings," said Donaldo. "This sort of trust protects our client's assets from the spouse's creditors, among other things, by limiting the spouse's access to those assets."

"So, if say, a husband owed a bunch of money

to loan sharks, they couldn't get to his wife's dough, right?" asked Wilson.

"Well, I guess you could put it that way," sniffed Oskowitz.

"Why in hell didn't you set up this spendthrifter account a long time ago?" I asked.

"**Spendthrift trust**," corrected Oskowitz, whom I immediately envisioned with a bullet hole in his forehead.

"Actually, detective, that is a very good question," said Donaldo. "We advised her to do it for years. We wanted to make her daughter the trustee of a spendthrift trust. Samantha is very sharp, as I'm sure you noticed. But, Kathryn knew that if Samantha stood between her desperate husband and her money, it might cause conflicts between the two. So, she had refused to protect her money from him, until reconsidering that form of trust just in the last few months before her death. In fact, we had set up a meeting for later this month to have her sign the papers for the spendthrift trust, but, as you know, that meeting will never happen now."

Wilson and I took a couple minutes to wrap our brains around his explanation.

"So, Fred will inherit all of her dough?" asked Wilson.

"Most of it," said Donaldo. "She recently had us make provisions in her will to assure that her daughter will inherit a considerable sum as well."

"Okay, so just how much money are we talking about in Mrs. Montgomery's estate?" I asked. "I mean, Fred Montgomery had a few drinks at his country club and made comments about his wife getting richer every day. Was that just booze talk, or is there truth in that?"

Here's the thing about financial guys, they love to talk about how rich their clients are, but most of the time they can't say a word because they don't want to be sued for violating their contracts and whatever ethics they might claim to have. So, once a wealthy client dies and they are facing subpoenas in a murder investigation, even the most tight-lipped number crunchers tend to sing.

"When Mr. Montgomery said his wife was getting richer every day, he wasn't exaggerating," said Donaldo. "Over the years, she has inherited nearly twenty million dollars from her family's estate, which has grown considerably thanks to our guidance. Most people could live like royalty just off the interest she was earning from her investments in stocks, bonds, and real estate."

"And then there was her most recent inheritance," added Oskowitz, who must have been feeling neglected.

"Oh? Please share more with the class," Wilson said.

"Kathryn had an unmarried aunt who died recently, and our client learned a couple weeks ago that the aunt had left her another nine million in assets," Oskowitz said. "According to Kathryn's will, Samantha will inherit that full amount."

"Nine million?" said Wilson. "Wow, I need to be nicer to my aunties."

Donaldo and Oskowitz were not impressed with my partner's attempt at sarcasm, but they weren't done sharing information.

"You might want to know also that Mr. Montgomery visited us shortly after his wife's murder, inquiring as to whether he could withdraw money from her accounts with us," said Donaldo. "We told him that Mrs. Montgomery's funds were not accessible to him at that point. Mr. Montgomery was not pleased at that news."

With that bit of information, we thanked them,

and they hustled us out the door. I'm sure they dialed up their attorneys as soon as we left the parking lot.

"Well, Fred, you piece of shit, now we know that you had at least twenty million reasons to want your wife dead," I said to Wilson in the car. "I shudder to think what might happen to Samantha if he blows through that and needs more dough. She might want to hire a bodyguard—or two or three."

Wilson shook his head at that.

"I don't see him as a killer, or at least, not as the guy who pulled the trigger," he said. "If he hired a professional to do the hit, which seems within the realm of reason, we need to get that figured out. Your identification of the ammo might help us do that. The use of wadcutters in a murder is rare enough that other cops would remember a professional hit where six kill shots were fired and there was no detectable trace of the ammo."

As we drove back to headquarters, Wilson and I talked about the Montgomery case, a homicide that was unusual in some ways, but all too familiar in others.

"Hey, Kenda, did you ever get so mad at your wife that you wanted her dead?"

"Naw, but if you asked her that same question about me, you might get a different answer."

"Yeah, well, I've wanted to shoot you a couple times myself, and we haven't been together nearly as long as you and Kathy."

"One thing about this job, you learn from the mistakes of others," I said. "As a patrolman, I was always getting sent out on domestic disturbance calls, and most of the time, the couple was fighting over some stupid little thing and then the argument just blew up into a major battle because they lost control and started pushing each other's buttons. I saw so much of that, I learned that when Kathy and I get to the breaking point, I just get the hell out of the house and go for a long drive, and I don't come home until I've got it under control again."

"Yeah, I do the same with Maggie. She's so damn smart, I don't even try to argue with her because she can make me lose my mind. I don't want to go there. I always think about the Pepsi bottle guy. I never want to go berserk like that!"

Wilson was talking about one of the most violent husband-wife murders we'd ever handled. This domestic dispute started out like most of them, a verbal argument over some minor issue that escalated into violence, and then became a crime not so much of passion, but of sheer blind rage.

These murders are often the most violent cases, with huge amounts of overkill; multiple gunshots or stab wounds, or spouses beaten to a pulp with a chair leg or a heavy bookend. Most humans manage to keep their emotions in check, but when they lose control in matters of the heart, you see the most violent forces within us take over.

The Pepsi guy collected antique Pepsi bottles made of heavy glass back in the days when they were sold from vending machines and could break easily if they weren't strong enough to take the beating from being banged around when dropped into the delivery chute. He had more than a hundred of them on display in their house. During a blowup with his wife, he just lost it, grabbed a hefty sixteen-ounce bottle, and hit her repeatedly in the head and face until she was dead, and probably after she was dead.

When we arrived, she was no longer recognizable as a female—or a human. The television set and wall behind it were covered with brain matter. We found the husband handcuffed to a sofa by the patrol officers who were first on the scene. He was still in the throes of a psychotic episode, still raging, but also asking, "Did I hurt my wife? Is she going to be okay?"

He'd gone batshit crazy with rage.

"Uxoricide!" said Wilson.

"Excuse me?" I said.

"Uxoricide is the term for the murder of a wife by a husband," he said. "I learned that from my high school English teacher Mr. McKenzie, while we were studying Shakespeare. He gave me a D on that test, the bastard!"

"Did the test include Shakespeare's line about murder?" I countered. "'**I kissed thee, ere, I killed thee**'? That's the only Shakespeare line I remember, so don't ask me for any others."

"Yeah, I guess husbands and wives battling each other were a big part of his schtick," said Wilson. "I'm married to a woman who cuts up bodies for a living, so I don't ever let our arguments get that far. Besides, as coroner, she could declare me dead and have my body turned to ashes before anyone knew I was missing."

"Ha! That's true. Kathy is a nurse, and she could probably find fifty ways to put me out of her misery if I pissed her off enough. I've never yelled at her or raised a hand to her, but I almost punched the wall one time during a stupid argument over something as important as which one of us forgot to buy soap at the grocery store. I was so pissed off, I turned away from her to hit the wall, and then I stopped and just walked out the door and went for my long drive. Later, she asked me why I didn't punch the wall and I told her, 'Because I didn't want to have to fix it.'"

"Long drives are a good idea, just don't stop at a bar; that's never a good idea when you are having a fight with the wife," said Wilson.

"Agreed," I said. "Driving requires me to focus on a normal activity and cools me off after an argument. Then, once I'm calmed down, I can go home like a grown-up and say I'm sorry for being such a dumb son of a bitch. Then we go to bed and make up. That's the best part!"

"I told Maggie that when I leave during an argument I dream about coming back, opening the door, and finding her waiting for me, dressed in a sexy negligee and looking like Brenda Lee while singing, 'I'm sorry, so sorry, that I was such a fool . . .' But so far, she hasn't taken the hint, dammit!"

As we pulled into the parking lot at police headquarters, Wilson returned to the uxoricide at hand, laying out our next steps in the Montgomery investigation.

"First off, you get to fill out an RIMN form—sorry kid, rank has its privileges—so we can submit them and see if any other jurisdictions have had murder cases involving disappearing ammo, six close-range kill shots, and a crime scene cleaner than my grandmother's kitchen," he said. "And then, we need to get our asses to Vegas and look for any holes in Fred's alibi, or any connections he might have made with a professional hit man. I'm sure Vegas is crawling with them."

PAPERWORK PAYOFF

Any cop, from desk sergeants and patrol officers to Vice squad detectives and homicide investigators, will tell you that paperwork is the bane of our existence. Few of us aced English composition or spelling. Nobody likes spending hours typing up reports that are scrutinized by superiors and, worse, defense attorneys and the media.

When Detective Wilson told me to fill out an RMIN form, he did not need to apologize, even though some might have thought of it as grunt work. We needed a break on the Montgomery case, and I was hoping that the RMIN form might lead to one.

RMIN stands for the Rocky Mountain

Information Network. Back in 1975, before the internet created instant ways to share information, the RMIN was our way of connecting with more than nine thousand other local, state, federal, and tribal law enforcement and public safety organizations in the United States, Canada, and Europe.

Think of it not as a Facebook group, but more of a Casebook group. We weren't sharing information about our cats, our favorite movies, or our social lives. Instead, I filled out a long form that gave the details of the Montgomery case, including Mrs. Montgomery's six lethal wounds and the type of weapon and ammunition used to kill her.

The goal is to inform others in law enforcement about your investigation just in case some other RMIN members might have had murders in which the same suspects, weapons, ammunition, or methods were involved.

When you submit a form, it can feel like a cry for help in the darkness. Most of the time, you don't get any responses. This was not one of those times. In fact, Wilson and I were stunned at the number of other detectives who contacted us because the Montgomery murder had striking similarities to their own cases.

"Good God almighty, Kenda the kid, you hit paydirt with that RMIN filing," Wilson said. "And several of these other cases aren't just similar in generic ways; a few of them have the same type of victim, the same number of lethal wounds, the same 'clean' crime scene, and, probably, the same type of weapon and magically disappearing ammo!"

The next day, the chief heard from the FBI agent in charge of the Colorado Springs office, John Vicars.

The chief brought Wilson and me into his office to listen on his desk phone speaker.

"You boys rang some bells with that Montgomery case," Agent Vicars said. "We need to keep this on the down-low for now. No media. I repeat, **no media**. But so far, we've heard from homicide detectives in San Diego, Salt Lake City, and Seattle. All of them have cases in which wealthy married women were murdered in their homes. All look to be professional hits. All were killed by six lethal shots at close range from revolvers with ammunition that left only minute traces of lead in the bodies."

After the call, our chief reminded us to keep the lid on this one.

"We don't want half the country stirred up with the media screaming about a serial killer running amok killing rich women," he said. "So, keep a low profile on this. Take the weekend off, but on Monday, I want you to contact every police department involved in those other killings to see what connections can be made to our case."

"But, Chief, you and I both know that it's better to just show up at their departments, offer to buy them dinner and drinks, and then ask about their cases," argued Wilson. "Most detectives don't have time to sit on the phone and walk us through their cases."

"Yeah, I know that, Wilson, but we don't have the fucking budget to send you all over the damned country right now," said the chief. "So, unless you got the cash, shut up and follow orders."

Wilson and I didn't take the weekend off. We met at his house on Saturday to have a few beers, and, mostly, talk through this latest development in the Montgomery case. If we really were dealing with some sort of serial killer hit man, we had a whole lot more ground to cover than with just a local murder.

We were three beers into our brainstorming session when Maggie made a rare appearance in Wilson's man cave. She came with a bowl of pretzels and a message.

"Hey, guys, the police chief called a few minutes ago. He didn't want to interrupt your little rumpus room party, but he said you should come in Monday without hangovers and wearing your shiniest suits."

"I wonder what that's about?" I said.

"The chief said Interpol and the FBI sent an alert about a known contract killer who is on his way to Colorado Springs," Maggie said. "They are coming in for a meeting."

CHAPTER TEN

THE CAPTAIN

SUNDAY, AUGUST 3, 1975

After jogging two laps on the five-mile running loop along the Thames River embankment, retired SAS officer Laurence Haywood, a.k.a. "the Captain," returned to his posh Richmond condominium, took a hot shower and a Numorphan pill to ease the pain along the scar in his right thigh. He then prepared his usual fry-up breakfast plate.

He dispatched the fried eggs, sausages, back bacon, tomatoes, mushrooms, bread, and black pudding while reading the **Sunday Times**. A story on the Helsinki Accords holding Communist nations to commitments on human rights briefly caught his attention. He chuckled when the story noted that the plane carrying US President Gerald Ford to Helsinki had wandered into restricted air space over Sweden and the Swedes had scrambled a jet to intercept and turn it away.

A Swedish Air Force major told the **Times** that their fighter was equipped with air-to-air missiles, "But, of course, there were no plans to use them on Air Force One."

This American president always seems to be on the edge of crashing even though he was supposedly quite the athlete, thought Haywood.

He read through the world and national news sections, then turned to the **Times** personal ads, a habit he'd developed during his "freelance" career after the military. The agents who connected him to clients used the **Times** personal ads to contact Haywood anonymously, but he'd been laying low the last year and had informed them that he was out of service, perhaps permanently.

Haywood was surprised then when he saw the coded ad addressed to him among the usual sundry collection of classifieds seeking lost pets, love connections, and vacation rentals.

Captain XX, please call Liz. All is forgiven, and your status honored. Sunshine is in your future.

How interesting, he thought. **Have my American friends forgotten that I am enjoying a hiatus and contemplating retirement?**

By arrangement, there was no phone number or other contact information provided on the personal ad. Haywood knew the phone number. It was a private Las Vegas number.

He finished his breakfast, cleaned up, and then stood on his balcony offering views of the Thames.

I thought I made it clear that I was out. I've had enough of doing their dirty business. More than enough.

Haywood believed in government service, but after many years of it, he had become disenchanted with serving at the whim of politicians and leaders with their own agendas. He'd done his duty, first with the D Squadron Twenty-Second Special Air Service regiment. Then, on to Cyprus with the United Nation's so-called "peacekeeping force." Then Borneo and South Arabia and all that nasty business with the covert, counterinsurgency Mobile

Reaction Force. He'd worked in the field recruiting 'Freds,' double agents in the ranks of the IRA, and, when the orders came, tracking and killing IRA leaders and other official designated targets.

The blurred battle lines with the IRA disturbed him. For the first time, he wondered if he was fighting for the right side, and then he was tagged for special black ops with the Revolutionary Warfare Wing working with MI6, in a special unit known as "the Armory." They worked in plainclothes most of the time, and a lot of the assignments troubled him.

I'm all for God and country, but I felt like a pawn, stirring shit up in other countries, taking out targets for murky purposes. I've had enough.

The government and military were using him to accomplish goals he no longer believed in. After breaking ties with them, he needed to find a source of income. His expertise didn't exactly qualify him for a desk job, but it wasn't long before people came to him, offering crazy money for his services.

"How do these people find me?" he wondered.

Haywood had friends and fellow soldiers from the SAS and special forces units from other countries who had become hired killers, mercenaries, or taken jobs with "private security" firms. They proved to be the source of his referrals. If one of them was offered an assignment and could not take it, they would suggest him as an alternative.

Every profession or trade has a network, so why not mine? But I had no idea there would be such a great demand out there. The "peaceful" world is far more bloodthirsty than the military world, it seems.

His first freelance assignment was eye-opening, which was remarkable considering that Haywood had already seen more than any man should have seen in his SAS missions. Another SAS veteran recruited him to take an assignment from Special Operations Group Ltd., a British company he'd never heard of until their brochure showed up in his mail after he signed on.

The contents made it sound like an insurance company or some sort of waste disposal operation. "We combine best-in-class brands, assets, and people within the complex nonfinancial risk management industry, offering turnkey solutions to address our customers' most complex challenges wherever they are needed around the world."

As it turned out, disposal—human disposal—was definitely part of the job. That first assignment from

Special Operations Group Ltd. involved a series of political assassinations in the most volatile corners of the Middle East. Haywood took a handful of other high-paying assignments on the African continent, China, and Afghanistan.

His diverse teams consisted of former members of the SAS, England's MI6, Israel's Mossad, the CIA, US special forces including SEALs, Green Berets, and Marine Force Recon, as well as others from the French Foreign Legion and Germany's Fernspaher long-distance reconnaissance unit, and that country's elite GSG 9 federal police force, which was created after the hostage crisis during the 1972 Munich Olympic Games.

Once he had saved up enough funds to support himself indefinitely, Haywood informed Special Operations Group contacts that he would no longer be available for their missions, but by then, his name had made some sort of black-ops-for-hire list that seemed to have circulated around the globe. More offers for "wet work" came to him. Some contacted him by telephone. Others by mail. Every now and then, a stranger would stop him on the street or knock at his door and hand over an envelope with contact information.

These were solo jobs, high-risk, and incredibly lucrative. He accepted those that targeted individuals whose deaths or disappearances were beneficial to the world in general—and inevitable, given their histories.

Men trained at his level, with his depth of experience, who were not insane headcases, drunks, or drug addicts, were a rarity. Those who were reliable and disciplined constituted a small fraternity. As a result, Haywood had more work than he could handle for the first two years. His retirement fund grew beyond anything he'd ever dreamed.

Then, his military service in Northern Ireland caught up with him. After his retirement from the SAS, Haywood had managed to cut all ties to his fellow operatives and the leadership in his unit. When he became a contract worker, he had moved to Grenada where he bought a two-bedroom villa in St. George's with a red tile roof overlooking Carenage Harbor and Port Louis Marina. He adopted a new identity as John Sandiford, a retired accountant.

For a few years, the British government lost track of his whereabouts. But then, about a year in Grenada, his past caught up with him and so did his former superiors.

Haywood was showering at his home after a morning run on the beach when a bomb placed just outside his closed bathroom door destroyed his villa. His body was propelled out of the shower and through the bathroom wall of the decimated villa like a bullet fired from its chamber. The thick antique door to the bathroom was made of native mahogany, which likely saved his life. Even so, his injuries were substantial. He nearly died twice on the operating table at St. George's General Hospital.

It took him a year to walk again. He still could not raise his arms above his head. The ringing in his ears was relentless. Overcoming his addiction to painkillers was a long process. The psychological torment was unceasing.

It was another year before his memory of events leading up to the explosion returned, and even then, it was many months later before he connected all the dots. The bombing had all the markings of an IRA revenge attack. An investigation by British intelligence found remnants of the explosives often used by IRA operatives.

But how did they find me?

Then he remembered seeing an unfamiliar face

one afternoon at the Good Life Bar & Snackette, an open-air, tin roof shanty on Paradise Beach. It was a ramshackle local hangout, not a tourist joint. Haywood had been having a late afternoon rum at a picnic table while talking to the owner Mama Belle, an island native who was protective of her clientele.

"Is that Irish fellow at the end of the bar a friend of yours?" she had asked Haywood.

"I don't recognize him, Mama Belle, and I doubt that I have many friends from the Emerald Isle."

The Irishman left soon after that, and Haywood had not given him another thought.

He would later learn, through his intelligence connections that the man was Jake Lynskey, a former IRA foot soldier, who had retired to Grenada, too, mostly to avoid criminal prosecution back home.

Lynskey had recognized Haywood as the man who had killed his older brother Duff. Jake Lynskey was just a teenager when he watched in horror from his bedroom window as Duff, a bricklayer and bombmaker, was shot in the yard outside their Bogside home in Derry. A security light came on just as the killer stepped into the yard, and the boy got a clear glimpse of his face as he fired his weapon.

Months later, during an IRA meeting, Jake put a

name to that face when Haywood was identified as a member of the SAS's elite Mobile Reaction Force that had recruited and planted spies in the IRA and targeted members for assassination.

"Duff's killer is here in Grenada, I just saw him at Mama Belle's rum shop," said Lynskey in a call to IRA contacts in Derry after spotting Haywood in Grenada.

"Stay clear of him. He is too dangerous. We will send someone."

Three days later, Haywood was blown out of his shower stall.

As soon as travel was possible, Haywood had moved back to London for better therapy, both physical and psychological. He was still using the pseudonym John Sandiford, but the bombing in Grenada had received wide coverage in the European media, and a photograph from his driver's license was displayed in many of the stories. As a result, British intelligence officials identified him as a former member of an elite SAS unit who had disappeared.

MI6 learned that Haywood had grown wealthy as a mercenary and hired killer under various disguises. They had no proof that he'd killed anyone that wasn't worthy of death, so the decision was made by British intelligence to leave him alone and monitor his activities.

"From what we have uncovered, Haywood only takes assignments from bad guys wanting other bad guys taken out. They are usually in rival terrorist or criminal organizations, so, frankly, he has not killed anyone that we wouldn't have wanted killed ourselves," said a top MI6 official at an Interpol meeting. "There are other killers for hire, including many former military people, who aren't as discriminating as the Captain. My recommendation is that we leave him alone, for now, and keep an eye on his activities and connections. Who knows? We may need a man of his talents one day ourselves."

So Interpol kept his file open, and followed his every move, alerting law enforcement agencies to a potential threat wherever and whenever he traveled. Haywood, who had tailed hundreds of targets, spotted them easily.

"I rather enjoy the cat-and-mouse games, now that I'm just an old, retired fellow," Haywood told his London girlfriend, Kay Cristwell, a British bank executive who found his scars, and his past exploits, an essential part of his appeal.

She encouraged Haywood to respond to the personal ad, "just to see what this is all about."

Monday dawned, cold and rainy. Suddenly, the idea of getting out of London for a few days was all the more appealing. After another run along the river to clear his head, a hot shower, and a shot of Jameson Black in his coffee, Haywood pulled his desk phone close and dialed.

"Hello?"

"The Captain, responding to Liz and her personal ad. My heart is ready for a new love," he said, giving the code phrase assigned to him.

"The boss will get back to you in fifteen minutes. Same number?"

"Yes," the Captain said.

Exactly fifteen minutes later, his desk phone rang.

"Captain, so good to hear from you."

"Yes, thank you. I thought you understood that I am out of service for an extended period due to health reasons," Haywood said. "As you no doubt know, I am on the radar of Interpol, so I am somewhat compromised."

"Oh yes, I was aware of that, and it is exactly why we want you for this job, which I think you will find to be a far less taxing mission than

most. I am prepared to pay you twice the regular fee, just because I know you are enjoying retirement, comfortable financially, and not looking for work. And, I think you will find this location to be quite suitable for additional rest and rehabilitation. Don't they say that the dry mountain air has healing power?"

"Why yes, they do," the Captain said. "Please send the details and I will review them over the next few days and then give you my response. Goodbye."

"Thank you, Captain. Hope you are feeling better, and goodbye to you."

CHAPTER ELEVEN

SOLDIERS OF FORTUNE

Our police chief, Dan Morrissey, was a local kid who joined the US Marines and served in the Korean War. He came home with a chest full of medals, joined the force, and worked his way up. Hard as nails and well-respected, he started as a beat cop, and quickly proved adept on the streets and in the bureaucracy. He could play the political game as well as any of them, but the rank and file considered him a cop's cop. We stood tall in his presence.

Chief Morrissey was not one for needless drama, so after getting his message Saturday night, Wilson and I knew something big had come up. We made sure to report for duty early on Monday and headed directly to his office.

"The FBI gave me a little more info this morning. Interpol notified them over the weekend that a certain killer-for-hire is headed our way," he said.

"They have been monitoring this guy for quite a while. He is a former British SAS officer whose last assignment was within a special unit that tracked down and took out targeted members of the IRA in Northern Ireland. He retired from the SAS five years ago and severed all ties. Then, he dropped off the radar for a couple years until recently. Interpol has kept an eye on him ever since because they discovered that he's become a contract hit man working mostly for various governments, including our own."

"Why haven't they just locked him up?" I asked.

"The answer to that is above my pay grade. You can ask the FBI today at the meeting," said the chief.

"Well, isn't this an interesting coincidence?" Wilson said. "We suspect a hired gun might have killed Mrs. Montgomery, then we find out that at least three other jurisdictions have similar cases, and now a known hit man being tracked by Interpol has booked a flight to our fair city?"

"Sounds too good to be true, don't you think?" I said. "If this guy is a pro and he just took out Mrs.

Montgomery, why the hell would he risk showing up again, especially so soon?"

"Maybe he dropped something at the murder scene that he needs to pick up," Wilson said.

"I don't believe a pro like this would be that sloppy," I said.

"Everyone makes mistakes, my son," Wilson said. "That's why prisons are overcrowded."

"The FBI is coming in later today with some friends from England, Germany, and other interested parties, so we'll learn more from them," said the chief. "Try not to spill coffee on them or otherwise embarrass me, the department, or the USA."

We were at our desks waiting to meet with the chief when the United Nations parade marched by. Once they were all seated in the conference room, Wilson and I were summoned to join them.

The chief didn't bother with formal introductions; he just waved a hand and noted the agencies represented. The FBI sent their Colorado Springs agent-in-charge, John Vicars, and Special Agent Mary Carroll from his office. They were the only visitors we knew by name. We'd dealt with Vic and Carroll often. They were both old-school FBI. Straight arrows. Big Catholic families. Vic had a law degree from Notre Dame. Mary Carroll graduated across the street from the Golden Dome at St. Mary's College where, despite the heavy Catholic Church presence, she learned to curse like a longshoreman. On more than one occasion, I'd heard her unleash her favorite expression, "Bless me Father, but what the fuck?" (Now you see why we liked her.)

The rest of the meeting's attendees were not so much our cup of tea. England's MI6 was represented by a stiff upper lip who looked like he'd popped out of a Jaguar commercial. There was also an Interpol representative from DC, and a couple of CIA stiffs who seemed to have crept out of a hall closet. Most people think the CIA only operates overseas, but they have offices all over the US and case officers tracking people, mostly foreign officials and foreign intelligence operatives, all over the country.

Special Agent Vicars was our master of ceremonies.

"Gentlemen, I'll get to the point. With the help of our colleagues in Interpol, MI6, and the CIA, we have been tracking a professional assassin known as the Captain. His real name, at least when he was with the SAS, was Laurence Haywood, but he has booked a flight into Colorado Springs under an alias."

Wilson and I were the local yokels in the room.

We'd never heard of the mysterious Captain, while most of our visitors seemed to be familiar with him and his reputation.

Special Agent Vicars passed out packets containing a bio, photographs, and other materials on the Captain that were compiled and prepared for the meeting by Interpol and its affiliates in law enforcement around the world.

"For those who haven't been tracking this individual, as we have, for the last three years, the Captain is a former British SAS commando, who served all over the world. He is highly trained in weapons, hand-to-hand combat, interrogation, intelligence gathering, and asset recruitment. For several years after leaving the SAS, he was a mercenary and killer-for-hire.

"Just a year ago, we lost track of him. We thought he'd been killed or retired. Then, the IRA blew up his beachfront hideaway in Grenada and we got word when he was recovering from severe injuries and undergoing physical therapy back in London. He seems to have recovered. Now, sources tell us, he is headed for Colorado. We don't know why."

I raised my hand because I couldn't help myself.

"If you know this guy has killed people as a hired gun, why haven't you locked him up?"

I tried not to take the shaking heads and condescending looks to heart.

"Apparently, our colleagues in Interpol say they've never caught the Captain in the act of killing someone that they did not otherwise want him to kill—or care if he killed—if you get my drift," Vicars said, nodding to the Interpol representative in the room.

His drift bothered me, but I kept my mouth shut. He was dealing with a much bigger jurisdiction than mine. Welcome to the great big real world, more gray than black and white. I don't like gray much when it comes to homicides.

Vicars continued with his briefing.

"Given this news of the Captain flying into this area, Chief Morrissey and I have discussed the possibility that he was involved in the recent murder of Colorado Springs socialite and philanthropist Kathryn Montgomery," he said. "Her killing certainly looks like a professional hit, but, as noted, the Captain hasn't been known to target random civilians who have no geopolitical importance, or any ties to terrorist organizations or organized crime.

"There is also the question of why he would risk returning to Colorado if she was his kill. That does not seem like a prudent move for someone as careful and smart as the Captain."

Wilson raised his hand, which looked a little silly for a guy his size.

"Yes, Detective?"

"Mrs. Montgomery has a daughter in Aspen who stands to inherit a big portion of her mother's wealth," Wilson said. "Could her mother's killer now be going after her?"

Special Agent Vicars weighed that question for a moment.

"We can't rule that out, certainly, so you might want to alert her to a potential threat and have her either leave the state or beef up her security," he said. "Again, this sort of thing doesn't sound like the Captain's bag, from what we know about him. His targets are usually significant threats to national security—in one country or another, for one side or the other—or they are high-level criminals affiliated with a cartel or the mob, either the US or the Italian divisions."

I raised my hand, playing along with the rest of the class.

"Vic, do you know of any potential targets in our state who fit into either of those categories and might be on the Captain's hit list?"

"That's a good question, Detective Kenda. In fact, we have considered that the Captain might have received a contract to take out someone in the federal Witness Protection Program, a former member of an organized crime family who was flipped. He and his family are living in this area now, and so we are dispatching additional protection to him.

"I can't give you any more information on this individual other than to say he is critical to an ongoing federal investigation," said Vicars. "We will be working with other agencies, foreign and domestic, to monitor the Captain's actions as soon as his plane lands in Denver. Some of you will be participating in that surveillance. We will arrest him if, and when, he appears to be an immediate threat to anyone.

"One more thing," the FBI agent said. "The Captain rarely kills anyone up close like your recent victim in Colorado Springs. He is trained as a sniper, one of the best in that field. So, keep that in mind. He can set up for a kill at a considerable distance from the target. You are going to need an extended protection circle around the target."

"C'mon now, Vic. How far are we talkin' here?" asked Wilson.

One of the CIA crewcuts raised his hand and volunteered to answer that question.

"Roderick Smithson here, part of my job is to track foreign hit men and mercenaries for the agency, especially when they are working for international terrorist organizations, drug cartels, organized crime families, and foreign governments. In a previous life, I was a special forces sniper in Southeast Asia. From personal experience and some knowledge of the Captain's training and reputation, I'd say you should consider a protection circle perimeter that starts at least a half-mile out from the potential target, unless the target is living in a densely populated urban area."

"Damn, a half-mile kill shot, that would be impressive," said Wilson.

"Well, yes, but our job is to make sure it doesn't happen," said Vicars, ending the meeting. "I will put together a plan for monitoring the Captain every step of the way, from London to Colorado Springs, and then to wherever he goes. Chief Morrissey will provide manpower from his department, and we will keep the rest of you informed. If you have any questions, you know where to reach me. Thank you for coming today."

Later, Wilson and I met with the chief to talk about our roles in tracking the Captain when he arrived in Colorado Springs. I took that opportunity to ask the chief about something that had been bothering me.

"Call me naive, but I find it hard to understand how guys like this Captain can keep killing people even though they and their activities are tracked by law enforcement," I said. "This just seems crazy to me."

"I agree with you, Kenda. I'm all for locking up every professional hit man and mercenary that steps into our jurisdiction even if the guy is just hiking up Pikes Peak for the fun of it, but maybe that's why I'm just a police chief in a midsized American town and not the director of the CIA or head of MI6," said Chief Morrissey.

"Have you seen that new magazine, **Soldier of Fortune,** published in Boulder by a former Green Beret gung-ho chest beater?" Wilson said. "The magazine has classified ads looking for mercenaries or former special forces guys offering their services for hire. I thought the whole soldier of fortune thing was all bullshit until this case came along."

Chief Morrissey dug under a pile of papers on

his desk, pulled out a copy of **Soldier of Fortune,** and tossed it to me.

"Yeah, boys, I thought it was bullshit too, but I had a phone conversation about this topic the other day with that CIA guy at the meeting, Smithson, who isn't a bad guy, really," he said. "He described this big global subculture of former elite military unit veterans who often can't hold down jobs in the real world when they leave military service, so they become mercenaries and killers for hire."

Smithson told the chief that a high percentage of these guys are basically addicted to violence and the adrenaline rush of combat, and they can't function in a normal world. Many also suffer from lack of sleep, an inability to concentrate, and even hallucinations because of their military experiences.

"Korean vets like me called it 'shell shock,' and I've heard others describe it as 'battle fatigue,'" the chief said. "Whatever it is, a lot of these guys feel like they don't fit into normal society, so they go with what they know, selling their services to the highest bidders."

"I can't believe there is that big a market out there for these hired guns," I said.

"Smithson said a lot of them first go to work as

mercenaries in African countries where they hire out to either the sitting governments or the revolutionaries who want to overthrow them. Then when they get tired of living in the jungle and getting bitten by snakes, they join private security firms or take contract work as bodyguards for rich shitheads and celebrities. And then there are a select few who work as hired killers taking jobs for the highest bidders."

"So, I guess the classifieds in **Soldier of Fortune** are how they market their services?" I asked.

"Smithson said most get referrals from former military contacts around the world who have ties to the mob, or foreign intelligence agencies that want someone killed without having it traced to them."

"So, it's a little more sophisticated than someone sitting at a bar asking the guy next to him to knock off his wife, right?" Wilson said with a laugh.

"Oh, you're talking about the Carl Perry case, aren't you?" the chief said.

THE HIT MAN COP

This was a legendary case in our police department. A guy named Carl Perry had soaked up five or six whiskeys with beer chasers at Nolan's Bar & Grill in our fair city and began yammering about wanting to hire someone to kill his wife. He poked the guy next to him and asked if he could help him do the job.

That guy was a retired city detective, Dominick Rodino, who played along, thinking Perry wasn't serious, just drunk.

"Yeah, I might know a guy who knows a guy, but it would be expensive," Rodino said, playing with him. "How much can you pay?"

"I'd pay at least five grand," Perry said.

Even then, Rodino was inclined to let it slide, thinking it was just the booze talking. When Perry kept bugging him, he said, "Meet me here for lunch tomorrow, sober, and we'll discuss this further."

Rodino thought that would be the end of it, but the next day, Perry showed up, and he was sober.

"If your guy can't do it, I heard about another guy in Denver," he told the retired cop. "I really need to get this done before the bitch takes all my money."

So Rodino came into headquarters and told Chief Morrissey about the guy in the bar who wanted to hire a killer and off his wife.

"I was inclined to just laugh it off, but then he said if I didn't help him he'd find somebody else, and he's talking enough money that somebody would probably do it, Chief, right?"

"You are right, we can't ignore this. We need to get ahead of it and make sure this Perry fella doesn't get his wife killed," said Chief Morrissey. "I'll have our detectives set up a sting. We'll have one of our guys pretend to be the killer-for-hire. He can wear a wire and gather what we need to put Mr. Perry behind bars. Sounds like that's where he deserves to be anyway."

The chief had looked up Perry to see if he had a criminal record. He'd scored a couple of aggravated battery charges, a DUI, and, on top of that, the department had a long record of complaints filed by his wife about being beaten and terrorized by him.

"Sounds good, Chief. Do you want me to set up a meeting between Perry and your fake killer?"

"Sure, and I think you will like the guy I'm casting in that starring role."

"Who's that?"

"Your grandson, Dino. He is such a ham, he'll be perfect!"

"Oh, Jesus, Mary, and Joseph, my wife will have a fit if she hears about this. But I'm sure Dino will kill it, so to speak!"

Robert "Dino" Fasano, Rodino's grandson, was a third-year detective and already a legend in our police department. He had a pile of black wavy hair and the dark good looks of a movie star as well as the toned musculature of an NFL linebacker thanks to many hours spent in the department's weight room.

Dino was a tough guy and looked like it, but he was also a prankster with a little kid's "hee-hee-hee" laugh. He was known for pulling chairs out from under the desk sergeants when they were trying to sit down, and for hiding pieces of paper in the lunch sandwiches of his fellow officers.

Aside from the "Dino" nickname handed down from his grandfather, Detective Fasano also was known as "Tarzan" because the king of the jungle was his childhood hero. When his grandfather was still on the department, he often regaled other cops with stories of the kid swinging on tree limbs and driving the nuns at his school crazy while practicing his Tarzan call on the playground.

When offered the starring role in the killer-for-hire sting operation, Dino stepped up, as expected. His grandfather arranged a meeting between Perry and the fake hit man at Nolan's dive bar. The place had been cleared of civilians earlier in case something went sour. Every patron in the bar was a cop dressed in street clothes and fully armed.

Dino was wearing a hidden body microphone under his shirt that was broadcasting to a receiver and recorder in an unmarked van parked outside. Wilson was one of the detectives in the van, along with an assistant district attorney who was there to make sure Perry gave us enough for a conviction on solicitation to commit first-degree murder, and a long prison term.

"It was great! At first Dino played it very cool to make sure Perry was serious about following through with it, but after he repeatedly said he wanted his wife murdered, Dino turned up the heat," Wilson said, picking up the story.

Wilson had shared this tale with me probably fifty times already, but I still enjoyed hearing it, almost as much as he enjoyed telling it.

"Okay, so for five grand, with half up front and half after she's dead, you can choose how I take her out," Dino told Perry.

"What do you mean? Just shoot the bitch and get it over with."

"Well, if that's what you want, sure," Dino said. "I thought maybe you'd want her to suffer a little considering she's made your life so miserable. I could make it a slow death, you know, by gouging her a couple dozen times, just enough to get her bleeding good. Or I could yank out a few fingernails and dunk her head in the toilet a few times before drowning her?"

"I don't know, I think shooting her will be enough, but make sure she sees it coming and the bullet goes right between her eyes!"

"A bullet to the brain will work," Dino said. "Should I make her strip naked and run around the house first?"

Wilson whooped as he delivered that line, which had become legendary in our department.

"Dino the ham damn near spoiled the sting with that question," Wilson said. "All the undercover cops in the bar were losing it. Some of them choked on their drinks. I was in the van, rolling around on the floor laughing my ass off."

When the DA signaled that we had enough on the tape for a conviction, Dino stood up, grabbed Perry, and pinned him to the floor while cuffing him and reading him his rights.

"Then he walked him out of the bar to a standing ovation and cries of 'Bravo! Bravo!'" Wilson said, finishing the tale with his usual flourish.

The chief laughed along like he'd never heard it

before either. Then, before ending the meeting, he got serious.

"I love that story, but I want to remind you that Carl Perry was just a local loser and a sap. He went down easy. This Captain is a whole different animal. We don't even know for sure who he is targeting, or if he even has a target. Just keep in mind, he is, by all accounts, an extremely dangerous man. Do not, I repeat, **do not** let him get the drop on you."

CHAPTER TWELVE

THE TARGET

Luca De Vecchio, a.k.a. Gio Gamboni, a.k.a. "Big G," was not happy when the US Marshals Service, under orders from the FBI, put him on home confinement until further notice.

"What the fuck, I paid a fortune for tickets to the PGA Tournament of Players Championship that starts on August 21 in Fort Worth. I bet ten grand that Nicklaus is going to repeat as the winner, and I spent another three grand on prepaid reservations Thursday through Sunday at the swankiest hotel in that cow town!" he said, screaming at his US Marshal security guards.

"We are just trying to protect your ass, that is all I can tell you," said Deputy US Marshal Jim Marno who led the mobster's security team. "Trust me, I'd rather be going to the game too."

Deputy Marno was just a year out of the US Marshals National Training Academy and wondering why the hell he didn't take the desk job with Traveler's, the insurance company that had offered him a job after college. He'd joined the Marshals Service envisioning a life of adventure, chasing bad guys across the country, but he'd spent the last nine months babysitting a mob rat in his Colorado McMansion.

"This is almost as bad as working at McDonald's, it's so freaking dull. The only thing keeping me from dying of boredom is the new Mrs. De Vecchio and the bags of donuts she brings me twice a week," he told his buddies from the Academy who seemed to have landed more interesting assignments.

"Yeah, well just don't be slipping her the long john," Marno's Training Academy roommate said. "That could get you fired, killed, or both."

"Ha! Don't worry, buddy. I'm very careful where I share the LJ. Besides, I've already seen her ducking into the pool house with their chef, Marco. He and the little vixen had better be careful. Her husband took down a bunch of mobsters, so he'd probably have no problem having them thrown off Pikes Peak."

Gio Gamboni made a fortune selling Sicilian-processed heroin as an off-menu item in his chain of twenty-five Big G Pizza Parlors up and down the East Coast. He was always careful to pay the required percentage of his profits to the Boston mob, which protected his operations. The Bostonian branch leaders were not so conscientious about passing on the required percentage of his fealty to the home office in Sicily.

This caused tensions. The Cosa Nostra don, Michele "White Mike" Bianco, countered by handing Gamboni to the feds on a silver platter, and then ordering him to sing to the FBI. Bianco banked on him providing enough damning dirt to wipe out the Boston mob leadership and clear the way for a new lineup handpicked by him and his Sicilian consigliere, Paolo Bertucci.

The plan worked. The top five bosses in Boston went up the river thanks to the newly created Racketeer Influenced and Corrupt Organizations Act (RICO) aimed at ongoing criminal enterprises in general and at heroin-dispensing pizza parlors in particular. Once the convicted Bostonians were locked away in their cushy federal prison cells, Bianco and Bertucci installed a new leadership of loyalists and immediately realized 30 percent increases in their ill-gotten gains.

In exchange for Gamboni's helpful testimony, the feds put him and his family in the Witness Protection Program. The grateful Cosa Nostra tossed in a supplemental protection plan against assassins hired by vengeful Boston mobsters and agreed to grant Big G ten wishes over ten years, if he survived that long.

"The Sicilians are like my fairy godfathers now, if fairies used sawed-off shotguns and Molotov cocktails," Big G told his new wife.

Thanks to the gratitude of both the US government and the Italian mafioso, the Gamboni family enjoyed a double layer of protection that was unique among those enrolled in the Witness Protection Program. Deputy US Marshals in bulletproof vests patrolled the inner courtyards and grounds of their Colorado compound while the outer perimeter beyond the walls was guarded by better-armed, better-paid, designer-camo outfitted security guards from Gold Shield Protective Services, under contract to a shell company owned by the Cosa Nostra.

The arrangement grew cozier than one might

imagine after a few months of blissful Colorado sun-shine. The two camps didn't exactly gather around a fire and sing "Kumbaya," but almost.

"Hey, we are both here from similar backgrounds and training, doing the same job, guarding the same people, so why can't we all just get along? If we work together, we can make sure everyone stays safe and even pool our resources," said Ben Paulson, a pri-vate contractor who'd served in the marines with three of the federal agents assigned to the Gamboni compound.

Over time, the two separate protection forces bonded. The low-paid government security staff and the mob's highly compensated private con-tractors sometimes split shifts and filled in for each other. In their off-hours, they skied together and lifted weights at the same fitness clubs. They even formed competing softball teams, the G-Men and the PC-Men, playing summer league tournaments with their girlfriends, wives, and kids watching in the stands.

In the first year of guarding Gamboni, two of the Deputy US Marshals quit and joined the Gold Shield security team for the better pay and bene-fits. None of the private contractors were tempted to join the FBI. "I couldn't take the wage cut," said Paulson. "I'd never be able to make the payments on my BMW."

They got along well because they had much in common. Most were veterans of the military and often from special forces units. Most were young, athletic, and easily bored. And nearly all shared a lust for Gamboni's alluring wife.

The retired mobster understood this, of course, and had even thought about adding a third layer of protection to keep his bodyguards' hands off his wife's lithe body.

"They think she married me for my money, but the truth is, she's more loaded than me now that I'm outta the heroin business," Big G told his eldest son, who was ten years older than the new Mrs. Gamboni.

The former Brandi Horowitz met the Pizza Connection drug trafficker while working the drive-up window at one of her father's Dunkin' Donuts franchises. She had just graduated from Arizona State University, where she was captain of the Sun Devil Spirit Squad Dance Team and majored in Sigma Nu frat boys with a minor in Phi Delts.

Upon matriculation, she lacked direction,

especially after her father cut off all financial aid. Hal Horowitz had gone for a late-night soaking in the family spa but found it occupied by two skinny dippers. One of them was his daughter Brandi, and the other was the pool boy, Raoul.

"You'd better find yourself a rich sugar daddy husband because I'm not giving you another cent," said the pissed-off father as he poured spermicide into his spa.

And so, Brandi accepted the invitation when the repulsive Gio Gamboni ordered a dozen chocolate éclairs and asked her out for dinner.

"What can I say? He had a cute bodyguard, and he was driving a Bentley convertible while wearing a pinky ring with a rock the size of a blueberry muffin!"

Within a month, Gamboni presented her with a three-carat engagement ring. Once he'd divorced his first wife and completed his testimony against the Boston mob, they were married in a small private ceremony guarded by more than a dozen federal agents. Brandi's father was so relieved to unload his wild-child daughter that he gifted her ten of his most lucrative Dunkin' Donuts franchises.

This wedding bonanza dramatically changed

Brandi's outlook on life. Before the surprise gift was bestowed upon her, she had resigned herself to at least ten years of bad sex and boring dinners. She figured it would take that long for her to screw her piggish spouse into a heart attack.

"I can't wait for the day when I never again have to scratch that fat hairy back," she told her garlic-scented young lover. "If I get lucky, maybe the Boston mobsters who survived the purge will come after him, but how they'll bust through the double wall of security, I have no frickin' idea."

Brandi might have looked like a trophy wife on the arm of the rotund and unreformed thug, but she was no fool. She had followed her father's advice and hired an experienced franchise operator to manage and grow her Dunkin' Donuts empire. They were cranking out nearly as much cash as Gamboni's former pizza chain without offering heroin as a side.

The money pouring in from her donut domain gave Brandi a new level of financial independence and freedom. Unfortunately, the Witness Protection Program and the Cosa Nostra supplemental security plan were cramping her style. Big G was also getting to be a pain in the ass. He hovered over her, screaming at her for flirting with both teams of security guards. He'd even had the nerve to accuse her of banging Marco the chef!

So, when informed that her husband was confined to quarters indefinitely due to a security alert, Brandi decided to spend the weekend at the Mountain View Resort's luxurious spa. "I'm gettin' dafuckouttahere!"

She had a quickie with Marco in the pantry before bidding Big G a fond farewell.

"Ciao, baby!" she said as she drove off in her Range Rover. "The next time you see me, I'll be even more fabulous!"

A MISSION GONE BAD

As Brandi drove off, the Deputy US Marshal in charge of her husband's security team, Jim Marno, watched from the guardhouse at the front of the driveway. "I guess I could have refused to let her leave, but her old man is our priority. She's such a damned distraction, parading around in her workout tights and shaking her booty all the time, it's probably a good thing she's getting the hell out of here. My guys need to keep blood flowing to their brains these next few days because we are clamping down and calling in more guns," he told Dano De-Pilotti, the leader of the Gold Shield team who had served in the marines with him for two tours in Vietnam.

"Why? What's up?"

"I just heard from the FBI agent in charge in Denver. He told me why they confined our guy Gamboni to the house this week. They got word that a high-end hit man known as the Captain is flying into Colorado Springs in the next couple days. They don't know where he is headed or what he is up to, but this guy is a serious threat."

"Yeah, I know him, strangely enough," said De-Pilotti.

"You do?"

"Remember that off-the-books rescue mission in Mexico I joined right after I was discharged and needed dough?" said DePilotti.

"Oh yeah, when a bunch of you went after the hippy kid from Austin that the Oaxaca cartel caught wandering around their weed-growing operation?"

"Right, well, the kid's old man, Lorenzo Garrido, owned the biggest barbecue place in Austin, a block from the UT football stadium. His twenty-year-old kid, Ricardo, had plans to open an authentic

Mexican-food joint next door to his father's place to catch the overflow of college students and Longhorn fans. He'd gone to the Oaxaca area looking for suppliers to provide local cheese and special wild tomatoes. Instead, he ran into a bunch of armed guys guarding the cartel's crop. They would have killed him then and there if one of the guards hadn't once worked in the kitchen of Garrido's restaurant. He recognized the kid and told his compadres that young Ricardo would probably bring a big ransom.

"They got a message to his old man, demanding five hundred thousand dollars for the return of the kid. Daddy was pissed off at his kid and didn't like being played by the cartel kidnappers. For him, it wasn't so much about the money. It was about those assholes demanding his money. Instead of just paying up, he stalled them by pretending to make a counteroffer for his kid at a lower price.

"While the kidnappers argued over whether to counter his counterdemand, the father contacted former marine friends in Austin connected to the gung-ho guys who published **Soldier of Fortune** magazine. They put out the call and recruited a team to go after the son.

"The Captain was the leader of the team. He

is British, former SAS. His real name is Laurence Haywood, and he is a badass. But on that mission, he ran into an even bigger and crazier badass who nearly took him out."

OAXACA, MEXICO, DECEMBER 1972

There hadn't been much time for training the motley crew of six mercenaries, but they were all military or law enforcement veterans, mostly marines and special forces. The only two non-Americans were the Captain and Bruno Kleiss, a former GSG 9 officer out of Bonn who had everyone looking over their shoulders. He was surly, kept to himself, and elicited concern even in this fierce group.

After they'd set up camp in a valley halfway between Oaxaca and the cartel's marijuana fields near San Pedro Totolapa, DePilotti went to the Captain, thinking they should cut the Kraut from the team.

"I don't know what the German's problem is, but nobody wants to partner with him," he said. "He is obviously well-trained, strong, and athletic as hell, but he's volatile, and I'm not sure he can be trusted to keep it under control."

"He's a psychopath. I've seen his kind before," said the Captain. "He's in this line of work because it gives him cover for hurting and killing people. But we didn't have time to be choosy, or to screen these guys, and he might prove useful against the cartel's security force. They'll be heavily armed and have at least three times the men. We can't afford to cut anyone."

"Okay, I'll partner with him and make sure he doesn't get us killed," DePilotti said.

"And watch your back with him," the Captain said. "He's a cunning cunt, that one."

The Captain had identified where the cartel was holding Garrido's kid, thanks to aerial photos provided by contacts in the Mexico City office of the US Bureau of Narcotics. The plan was to move through the marijuana fields at night, armed with M16 rifles and M60 machine guns fitted with starlight scopes for night vision. Lorenzo Garrido had found a former Vietnam pilot with a chopper to evacuate the kid once the Captain's team grabbed him and took him to the designated pickup zone. There wasn't room for the rescue team, so they'd have to drive out in the three Jeeps they'd been provided.

"We were supposed to move out at zero hundred hours, but the shit hit the fan about twenty-three hundred," DePilotti said. "I woke up and noticed

Bruno wasn't in the tent. I did a quick search around camp and couldn't find him. So, I woke the Captain and told him that the German might have gone AWOL. Then, I remembered that we'd driven through a small village just a couple clicks up the road from the camp and I'd seen Bruno staring at the women and their daughters in the market there. He was practically drooling."

The Captain and DePilotti drove a Jeep to the village. Upon arrival, they split up to search for him. The Captain found the German on top of a teen girl who appeared to be unconscious or dead. He grabbed Bruno by the collar and pulled him off the mutilated body.

The blade of Bruno's knife flashed in the moonlight as he came up off the girl. He spun and buried the knife in the Captain's right thigh, hitting his femoral artery. DePilotti showed up as the Captain went down. Bruno disappeared into the forest.

"The combat knife blade was still in the Captain's thigh," the marine recalled. "I dragged him to the Jeep, pulled out a first aid kit, and applied a tourniquet to keep pressure on the wound so he wouldn't bleed out. I called the chopper pilot on the radio and met him at the designated pickup place. I kept pressure on the Captain's leg and then turned him over to the ER doctors in a hospital in Mexico City. Somehow they managed to keep him alive and save his leg."

The mission to rescue Ricardo Garrido was aborted. His furious father coughed up the ransom instead—after negotiating it down to $250,000 and throwing in a bunch of coupons for free brisket and black bean dinners.

"I visited the Captain in the hospital during his recovery, and he told me that if he ever laid eyes on that fucking German psycho again, he'd blow his head off," DePilotti said.

"Wow, that's a crazy story," said the US Marshal security team leader, Deputy Marno. "But the Captain doesn't sound like a guy who'd take a job to kill a mob rat like Big G, does he?"

"From my experience with him in Mexico, I wouldn't have thought so, but you never know, sometimes guys get desperate for money, or they just become stone-cold killers with no scruples or conscience. I do know that if the Captain has a contract to kill Gamboni, we'll have one hell of a time stopping him. I've seen him shoot the eyes out of a potato from a half-mile away."

CHAPTER THIRTEEN

MISDIRECTION PLAY

THURSDAY, AUGUST 21, 1975

The Captain's British Airways flight departed from Heathrow Airport at 7:00 a.m. London time and landed at the Dallas Fort Worth Airport ten hours later. After a layover, he boarded an American Airlines flight to Colorado Springs and arrived at our airport at 8:00 p.m. Thursday.

Between the FBI, the CIA, MI6, and our department, we had him tailed each step of the way. If he peed on the plane, we heard every dribble. When the Captain entered the terminal—tall, lean, ruddy features, tweed sports coat, wool pants, and a carry-on bag—we had ten of our own waiting to track him within our jurisdiction.

We couldn't arrest the bastard because there were no warrants out or grounds for taking him into custody. All we could do was watch him.

"If he's packing a sniper rifle, it must be a handy-dandy fold-up model," Wilson said.

Wilson and I were stationed in the airport security room, monitoring a set of screens fed by security cameras.

"Damn, he's good," Wilson said. "I think he's already made Andrews at the check-in desk, and did you see him nod at Special Agent Mary Carroll as she followed him off the plane?"

"Oh shit, look, he's walking toward Michaels like he spotted an old friend," I said.

Logan Casey Michaels was a retired street cop recruited to join the surveillance team. He was posing as a janitor emptying trash cans in the terminal. We watched in horror as the ballsy Captain went up to Michaels, patted him on the shoulder, and said something before moving briskly toward the baggage area.

Later, Michaels filled us in: "He was really friendly, gave me a little pat and said, 'Hey ol' chap! You can tell your fellow officers that I'll be heading to the Hertz desk where I've reserved a blue Ford Bronco.

From there, I will be driving up to Aspen for a few days of exhilarating hiking, drinking, and eating. I hope some of you fellows can join me, the weather is supposed to be just smashing!'"

"Aspen? Oh shit, could he be targeting the Montgomerys' daughter next? But why would he tell us that he was headed that way?" Wilson said. "This is nuts, but I'd better call and tell the daughter to either find a secure place for her family before he gets there or to keep everyone tucked inside and away from windows."

"Okay, I'll notify the FBI of the potential threat in Aspen. They should send a team up there to guard that family while the Captain is in the area," I said. "We can't trust the Aspen cops to protect them. Most of them are too stoned to shoot straight."

The Captain picked up his Bronco at the Hertz counter as promised. A team led by the FBI was on him as soon as he pulled out of the parking lot. We sent a patrol officer to the Hertz counter to see what alias the Captain was using. The impressive fake driver's license was for J. Edgar Allen Poe of Washington, DC.

"You have to like a hired killer with a sense of humor," said Wilson.

"Or not," I replied.

We stayed in touch on a closed radio channel with the FBI agents tailing the Captain. They'd thought his target might be their mob snitch in Witness Protection who was stashed in Colorado Springs' swanky Mountain View neighborhood, so they were surprised when the hit man took the exit north to Denver after leaving our airport.

"Well, there goes that frickin' theory," said Agent Mary Carroll, who'd hopped on the Captain's flight during the Dallas layover before it headed to Colorado Springs and tailed him ever since. "We're headed to the Mile High City. Maybe he was telling the truth about Aspen. This is making my head spin, boys!"

"Just don't let the Captain blow it off your shoulders, M. C.," said Wilson, whose wife was pals with the FBI agent.

"Thanks for caring, Wilson!" she replied.

Agent Carroll called on the radio again three hours later. She sounded exhausted.

"Well, here's some weird shit," she said. "The Captain took a detour into the town of Golden, drove to a place called the Victorian Inn near the School of Mines campus, and checked in for the night."

"What's so strange about that, don't all hit men stay in B&Bs?" I said.

"It gets even stranger," said Agent Carroll. "Around midnight, he walked out of the inn and greeted this gorgeous young woman who'd just pulled into the parking lot," said the FBI agent. "They hugged, and then he helped bring her bags into the inn."

"Christ almighty," said Wilson. "What is this guy up to?"

"Hey, M. C.," I said, "did you get the make and license plate of the woman's car? Maybe we can figure out who she is."

"Yeah, I already ran a check. It's a rental from a Hertz location near the University of Colorado in Boulder. It was rented in the name of Lily Mae Haywood. She's twenty-one, and the address she gave is for a student apartment complex just off the CU campus."

"Wow, she must be the Captain's daughter. We had no idea that he had a family here. Keep us posted. This is getting more and more bizarre. There's no way he is taking his daughter on a hit. This is looking like a wild-goose chase for everyone involved," Wilson said.

"Maybe they are driving up to Aspen in the

morning after getting some sleep," I said. "If nothing else, you and your team can work on your downhill racing skills while you are up there."

"Funny . . . not! That's another weird thing. There's little to no snow in Aspen now. Hell, last time I checked, it was seventy-five degrees up there during the day," said Agent Carroll.

"Maybe they just want to look at the changing leaves on the Maroon Bells?" I said. "We've taken our kids up there a couple times to do that in the fall. You might get to watch a killer watch the leaves change. Exciting!"

"Well, I'd rather do that than get in a frickin' shootout with a veteran sniper slash assassin," Agent Carroll said. "I'll let you know where we end up tonight. So far, he hasn't tried to lose us, so it will be interesting to see how this goes down."

FATHER-DAUGHTER WEEKEND

"So, Dad, what's this trip all about?" asked Lily Mae Haywood the next morning as she and her father drove to Aspen. "I mean, I'm not complaining. I love Aspen in the fall, but I had to skip out on three days of classes to make this trip with you."

"Well, Lily Mae, all you need to know is that

my bosses are paying your father a princely sum to take a long weekend and check out one of the most beautiful mountain resort cities in the world, and I chose my favorite daughter to hang out with me."

"That's very nice of the Bank of London. What exactly do you do for them, again? Whatever it is, you must be making them a lot of money for them to spring for this trip. And I'm guessing you couldn't get your girlfriend to come?"

"Oh, Kay probably would have joined me, but since you were already in Colorado and I haven't seen you in a while, I thought this would make a good getaway for the two of us. Have you ever stayed at the Hotel Jerome?"

"No, Daddy dearest, that's a little out of my price range, unless of course you were to raise my monthly allowance!"

A CLEAR FIELD

With the Captain headed for the mountains under surveillance by the FBI, and with assurances that Samantha Montgomery Towers and her family were safely tucked away in Aspen, the chief told Wilson and me to take the weekend off and recharge.

"Unless the Captain surprises us and goes after

the Montgomerys' daughter, which would mean he's our guy, I want you two hitting that investigation hard next week," he said. "As much as I hate to spend our citizens' tax dollars, I think you need to go to Vegas and find out if Fred Montgomery had some sort of connection there that provided him with both an alibi and a hired gun."

Wilson and I went to our respective homes and our respective wives and crashed. This case was driving both of us to the brink of exhaustion. Kathy and I nodded off Sunday night while watching **The Best of Carson**. I woke up to Shelley Winters yammering at Johnny and thought I'd died and gone to hell. I shut off the television and dragged my wife to bed.

My head hit the pillow and I was out.

Then the damned phone rang.

"Kenda! Shake a leg and suit up! I'm on the way!"

"Fuck, Wilson, what is it, now?"

"It's Big G's wife! Someone took her and her boyfriend out in the sauna at the Mountain View Spa."

A FOND FAREWELL

Josef Jobst of Klesberg, Germany, had departed the Copenhagen Airport on a KLM flight at 9:44 a.m. Friday, and after stops in Amsterdam and Atlanta,

Georgia, he arrived at Denver's Stapleton International Airport eighteen hours later, on a Delta flight.

He rented a Ford Bronco 4×4 Explorer from Avis, using his counterfeit passport rendered by Herr Ernst. Bruno did not mind waiting two days for the passport to be completed because, as luck would have it, Roma was available and entirely willing to dominate his time, as well as his body.

Every time I see her, I am so glad I haven't killed her, which is so unlike me. Have I gone soft? I don't think so. I still love butchering a bitch on the side now and then. Maybe this is love, whatever the fuck that is. Can it be love if I'm paying for it?

The fresh bruises on his back made it difficult to get comfortable during his flight to the United States, but he used the pain to get focused for this assignment.

I never would return to the same city or state so soon after a kill, but they assured me that they had a plan to distract law enforcement and draw them away from my target's location.

Still, Bruno had flown into Denver's airport rather than the smaller airport in Colorado Springs just in case someone was still monitoring arrivals there. As he moved through Stapleton, secured his rental vehicle, and drove off, he picked up no signs of surveillance. Just to be sure, he drove west on the interstate for a few miles before making a U-turn on a service road. Then he made his way south to his designated target's location.

"Things have changed," said his Vegas connection when Bruno had made the required final check-in call at the Denver airport. "Your fee will be tripled. A second package will be at the pickup location, and you are to dispose of it, as well. Do it however you choose, but make it a fond farewell."

"I understand," said Bruno, smiling at the thought. He'd been informed in his initial instructions that the target had a lover who might also come into play.

A bitch with no morals, cheating on her husband with a scumbag he'd trusted. This will be far more gratifying than I'd expected. But I've got to keep it under control. Just follow the instructions, get in and get out. Stay professional on assignment. Feed the monster on your own time!

SPA DAY FROM HELL

Marco had surprised Brandi at the Mountain View

on Saturday night by stripping off his clothes and then slipping into the spa's steam room to join her.

"Marco! You are so naughty! If Gio knew you were here, he'd shoot you!"

"Fuck that old, fat swine! I took the weekend off. He can make his own calzone while his guards protect him. You are too beautiful to be left naked and alone."

Their foreplay progressed from the steam room into the sauna. They showered together afterward and moved to the plush massage room. They dismissed the masseuse with a fistful of cash. They had then polished off a bottle of Brunello di Montalcino smuggled in by a waiter whom Marco bribed to violate the spa's ban on alcohol.

Their lovemaking continued in front of the fireplace. Neither of them had heard the killer sneak into the room. Marco was on top of Brandi, and oblivious to the world he was about to exit.

Bruno slit his throat first.

Brandi's eyes flew open when she felt Marco's blood dripping on her neck and breasts, but Bruno's combat knife was across her throat before she could utter a word.

The killer watched in silence as the two of them gasped for air and then died. Standing over them, he cleaned the blood from his knife by swiping it with a thick Turkish towel bearing the Mountain View Spa name and logo.

No bullets for you two lovers in these surroundings, and besides, my blade was every bit as swift and efficient.

Bruno then pulled Marco's body off Brandi. A rush of pleasure ran through him as he viewed his swift and deadly handiwork. He felt another surge of adrenaline as he knelt over them and went about creating the "fond farewell" message requested by the client's representatives in Las Vegas.

ANOTHER UXORCIDE

The moonlit mass of Cheyenne Mountain came into view as we drove through the entrance onto the lush three-thousand-acre Mountain View property.

"Do you know that John Wayne used to stay here all the time?" Wilson said.

"Yep, I heard he ate all the shrimp off a waiter's tray while riding the service elevator on one visit," I said.

Wilson had to top that.

"Well, I know for a fact that he once rode a horse into the Golden Bee British Pub here."

"You gotta love the Duke," I said.

"Yep, Pilgrim, ya sure do!"

Wilson had taken a detour to pick me up, so Dr. Maggie beat us to the scene of the crime. The Mountain View's security had everything roped off. Better late than never.

Patrol Officer James Jordan was again first on the scene and stood waiting for us in front of the location.

"Top of the morning, gents. Coroner is here and the crime scene unit is on the way," Jordan said. "Your victims on this occasion include a twenty-five-year-old female and a thirty-two-year-old male. Only the female was registered to this hotel. You will find them in the massage room. It appears their killer first slit the throat of a room service waiter and took his universal key to gain entry to the spa area. We found the waiter's body stuffed in an industrial-sized dryer in the laundry room down the hall. Both victims in the massage room were killed in the same manner as the waiter, only they were naked."

"Thank you, Officer Jordan, we appreciate your succinct briefing, as always," I said. "Please keep all hounds at bay."

"Yes, sir, Detective Kenda. My pleasure."

The heat from a blazing wood fire behind the iron fireplace grate was intense. The exotic wood paneling glowed from the flames. All very cozy, except for the gore.

As we walked up, Dr. Medina pulled a bloody mass from the mouth of the late Mrs. Gamboni.

"My god in heaven," she said. "Just when I thought I'd seen it all."

Wilson and I didn't have to ask what the mass was, or where it came from. The male victim's mutilated crotch with a missing penis provided that answer.

"Looks like someone was not happy that these two were hooking up here at the lovely Mountain View," Wilson noted.

"You said a mouthful," I replied.

Dr. Medina shot me a look that might have knocked even John Wayne to the ground. Wilson pretended to ignore me because he didn't want to get locked out of the bedroom back home.

"Well, this could be the work of another pissed-off husband, but it doesn't have any of the same markings as the Montgomery murder," he said.

"If it was the same contract killer, he probably thought gunshots would bring too much attention in this situation," I said. "Most of the guests here are rich old bastards who couldn't hear a gunshot if it was in their hairy ears. But gunshots in a resort tend to get noticed. They have a big security team here. Half the guys on our force moonlight for it. They earn twice the department's hourly pay."

"Detectives, did you see this?" said Dr. Medina, stepping back from the bodies.

Once she moved aside, we could see where this killer, like Mrs. Montgomery's, had knelt in the blood next to the male while mutilating him. The imprint appeared to be much like the one found at the Montgomery crime scene.

"If it proves to be a knee print from another pair of Levi's 501 jeans, we can narrow the list down to a couple zillion suspects," I said.

"At least we know this wasn't the Captain's doing since the Bureau is tracking him," said Wilson.

"And besides, he's more of a tweed and wool chap," I added.

On the way to the Mountain View, we'd heard on the radio from Special Agent Carroll that she and her team were following the Captain and his young lady passenger out of Aspen and back toward Denver.

"All they did was hike around the mountain trails, hit a few shops, have a few drinks, and share lively banter over a bunch of expensive meals," M. C. said. "I can guarantee you that the only thing the Captain killed on this trip was a couple bottles of wine and the frickin' entire year's travel budget for the Bureau's Colorado Springs and Denver offices."

A FAMILIAR FACE

The Captain hugged his daughter, kissed her on the cheek, and then helped move her bags from the rented Bronco to her rental car in the B&B parking lot around 11:30 a.m. Monday morning.

"Study hard. Enjoy college. But don't talk to boys!" he told Lily Mae.

"Thanks, Daddio! I had a blast," she said.

Once he was back on the interstate and headed for the Denver airport, the Captain switched on the car radio and found a news station.

I have no idea why they paid me a fortune to make this trip, but I suspect they wanted me to draw the FBI up into the mountains for some reason. I think most of their Colorado agents accompanied us.

The noon newscast offered a potential clue for him.

"There has been a triple murder at the Mountain View Resort in Colorado Springs. Police say one employee and two guests, a man and a woman, were found stabbed to death at the Mountain View Spa overnight. No suspects have been arrested or identified. They have not released the names of the victims pending notification of their families. We will have more on this breaking news story as it develops."

The Captain was still mulling over that report and its implications as he returned his rental car at the airport and made his way to the departure gate for his flights, first to Atlanta, then on to New York City for a connection to Heathrow.

On his way through the international terminal, the Captain noted a long line of passengers moving into the gangway tunnel for a direct flight to Berlin, Germany. One of them stepping into the tunnel, a muscular male with close-cropped blond hair, wearing blue jeans and a tight-fitting shirt, struck him as familiar. More than anything, the Captain recognized the swagger as he disappeared down the ramp.

Bruno!

CHAPTER FOURTEEN

KILLER CONNECTIONS

We gladly stepped aside to let the FBI take over the triple murder investigation at the Mountain View Resort. They had jurisdiction since the late Mrs. Gamboni had been in the federal Witness Protection Program.

Chef Marco was considered collateral damage. Wrong place. Wrong time. And, the wrong woman married to the wrong guy.

"I have no doubt Big G knew about his wife and the chef and he ordered the hit, probably through his friends in the Sicilian mob," said Special Agent Vicars, chief of the FBI's Colorado Springs office, in a conference call with us.

"Of course, proving that happened won't be a walk

in the park. So, if you guys come up with anything pertaining to this case in your investigation, let us know."

"Other than it being a hit on a wealthy wife, this Mountain View case doesn't really seem to fit our killer's MO," said Wilson, "but we will certainly keep you informed."

"I'm beginning to think we should check the Yellow Pages for a Murder Your Wife Inc. listing," I said. "The Rich Dead Wives Club will be bigger than Rotary International if the murdered missuses keep dropping."

With distractions like the arrival of the Captain and the killings at the resort, Wilson and I hadn't had much of a chance to check in with the other police departments that had responded to our bulletin regarding the Montgomery case on the law enforcement information network.

In our alert that went out to other agencies around the world, we specified that we were looking for similar professional-type hits on married women in other jurisdictions. We had more than a dozen responses, but only three of them reported that the wives had been shot six times with ammunition that left little or no traces of lead in the body.

All three were in the western United States. All were in affluent areas. The other three we knew of so far were in or near Seattle, San Diego, and Salt Lake City. Ideally, Wilson and I would have visited each of the investigating police departments to talk in person with their investigators. It's a fact of life that most detectives are too damned busy with their own cases to stop what they are doing and walk someone through their investigations on the telephone.

"We shouldn't tell them we're coming because they'll tell us they don't have time," Wilson said. "We'll just show up, take them out for dinner and drinks, and win them over with our roguish charms."

Wilson was right. We needed to make eye contact, have a few beers—or at least a few cups of coffee—and establish trust by offering details of our case in exchange for information on theirs.

We went to the chief with our travel plan, and he shot it down with a bazooka.

"I know, I know, I fucking know. In a perfect world, you'd meet face-to-face with the other detectives. I get it," Chief Morrissey said. "But this is the real world, you work for the penny-pinching city of Colorado Springs. You aren't Gene Barry, millionaire city detective from **Burke's Law**, as far as I know. At least, I haven't seen your Rolls-Royce parked out front."

Wilson and I didn't push it. Real-world cops have to deal with real-world problems. The whole country was in a recession thanks to the oil crisis. City governments were struggling nationwide. The chief had to pick his fights with the city's bean counters.

"Look, I'm already trying to squeeze enough money out of the budget to send you to Vegas because that's the only way you can really check out Fred Montgomery's activities there, so just get what you can from these other cities by working the phones and then we'll send you to Sin City for a couple days."

Wilson and I weren't all that excited about driving all over hell anyway, so after our meeting with the chief, we retreated to the coffee room to regroup.

"I was gonna suggest that we get Fred Montgomery to cover our trip costs with all the millions he will score when his wife's estate is settled," Wilson joked.

"My guess is that Fred's long line of bookies and loan sharks are standing in line ahead of us," I said.

COLD CALLS

For the next week, we worked the phones, calling homicide detectives in Seattle, San Diego, and Salt Lake City. We left dozens of messages that were never answered, but we kept plugging. The first step was just getting to the names of the detectives handling the murdered-wife cases. Then we had to figure out what shifts they worked and when they'd be most inclined to pick up the phone and talk to us. If ever.

"San Diego PD, Homicide division, Detective Charles Berry speaking."

"Detective Berry, this is Detective Joe Kenda with the Colorado Springs Police Department, wondering if you have a minute to discuss the Bonnie Mortimore Smythe murder case because we have a similar case here . . ."

"I'm eatin'."

"Okay, well, when can I call you back?"

"Call me back when I ain't eatin'!"

Slam!

And so it went.

We'd keep plugging away until we'd either wear them down or they'd feel sorry for us. They'd all been in our shoes, busting their balls, just trying to make a case. Some would let us call them after hours at home when they could talk without pissing off a supervisor or getting dispatched to another homicide.

Eventually, we learned that all three of the other

murders had occurred in the three years prior to the Montgomery case. When we told them that our victim was shot with wadcutters, the detectives in San Diego and Seattle thought we were bullshitting them.

"Wadcutters? Never heard of 'em. Are you yanking my chain? What the hell are you smoking out there in the Rockies?"

But we got a more interesting response from a salty female detective in Salt Lake City named Ashley Douvikas. Before I even mentioned the number of wounds or type of ammo used on Mrs. Montgomery, she jumped in:

"Hey, hold on! Did your vic look like she'd been hit by a professional? Six kill shots to the brain and vitals? And did the shooter use frickin' wadcutters?" she asked.

"Why yes, he did," I replied. "How did you figure out it was wadcutters?"

"I spent half my childhood in Greece with my grandparents and my grandfather Alexander Constantine Douvikas belonged to a target-shooting club in Athens. He taught me to shoot, and we used wadcutters for paper targets because they left such a big hole—pretty much like those in our victim."

Thanks to Detective Douvikas, we had more reason to believe our killer was responsible for the other similar cases. We circled back to the San Diego and Seattle detectives, and, after some pissing and moaning, they dug out their reports and agreed that their killer had used the same modus operandi.

The location of the bullet wounds was the same for them all, give or take an inch or two. The use of wadcutters and the six kill shot pattern suggested that one hit man might be responsible for several homicides, but he was still a ghost. All we had was a thin bit of circumstantial evidence, and with thousands of rounds sold every day, well, we still were grasping at straws.

The husbands were primary suspects in each case, but every one of them had a solid alibi that placed them out of town when their wives were murdered. Access to the wife's substantial funds was an obvious motive in three of our four similar cases. One of the husbands was addicted to porn and hookers, and his heiress wife was threatening divorce. He was a mega-church preacher, so it was complicated.

The second husband was also under threat of divorce, but his chosen vice was cocaine. In the third case, the outlier, the wife wasn't the cash cow in the family, but she had caught her politician husband in bed with his male campaign aide and she had threatened to go public and destroy his career.

In each murder, the husband stood to benefit substantially by becoming a widower. After days of coaxing, okay, **begging**, we convinced our fellow detectives to send us copies of their case reports, including interviews with the husbands and others related to the investigations. We pored over those reports and called some of the people to talk to them ourselves.

"You never see Jack Lord working the phones night and day on **Hawaii Five-O**," I told Wilson as we ended our fourth week of calls.

"Hell no, he always let his lackey Dano do all the damned grunt work," Wilson said. "I'm getting cauliflower ear from being on the damned telephone all day and all night."

A few days later, I was on the phone with a sister of the Seattle area murder victim Jenny Debb when a couple of my muddled brain's neurons connected and ignited a thought.

"My sister was planning on divorcing the asshole, but he had her killed first," said Mary Sue Green. "She'd found out that her husband had a boyfriend in Vegas. She thought he only cheated at gambling. Turns out, he was a multifaceted, cheating son of a bitch."

The mention of Vegas was the spark. It kept coming up in our conversations with the victim's friends and families. Fred Montgomery was a frequent Vegas visitor, and so were the husbands of the victims in San Diego and Salt Lake City.

"Looks like we have another couple reasons to visit Sin City, Kenda my lad," Wilson said. "You ready to hit the Strip?"

"Hell no. Never been there. Never wanted to go there," I said. "I work too damned hard for my money to hand it over to some mob boss casino owner."

THE VEGAS CONNECTION

Every major city has an underworld of thieves, pimps, drug dealers, and other small-time crooks who do the dirty work of the criminal hierarchy even as it preys upon them. Most of the low-level mopes are idiots who spend as much time locked up as on the streets. None of them can be trusted except to be untrustworthy.

Las Vegas was the major league of the underworld

when we visited for this case in 1975. Crime was paying well on every level there. Of course, the mob was making most of the money. The founding father of crime in Vegas, Bugsy Siegel, was long gone, but the Chicago mob had installed a thug named Anthony Spilotro to keep the taps flowing. The Syndicate was raking in millions from the Vegas Strip. Street-crew bosses who could keep the cash flowing were considered the entrepreneurial class. If you had a mob connection—even if you just knew a guy who knew a guy—you were golden.

The FBI had their hands full in Vegas, always scrambling to keep up. Their agents used the underworld's petty criminals as a labor pool too. They held their feet to the flames or paid them monthly snitch fees to serve as informants. The FBI's goal was always to go after the biggest target possible.

We touched base with the local office of the Bureau when we arrived in Vegas, but we figured they'd probably blow us off. Instead, we called upon my friends the Birch brothers, who'd been helping me track Fred Montgomery's activities in Vegas.

Doug was a lieutenant in charge of the Vice division for the Las Vegas Police Department. His big brother, Lenny, was a federal Organized Crime

Task Force agent using the alias "Lenny Blackbear" while working undercover on the security team at the Whitehorse Casino. The brothers kept the fact that they were siblings a secret since having a brother on the local police force might have raised suspicions among Lenny's mob bosses and coworkers.

"Of course, a high percentage of the cops here are on the mob payroll, so it probably wouldn't make all that much difference," said Lieutenant Birch.

The Birch boys didn't hang out together in public because side by side, they looked like brothers. They were an imposing pair, built like NFL linemen. Doug was six foot six. Lenny was six eight. Both had black hair, black eyes, and facial features that gave away their heritage, which Lenny described as "part Seminole, part Sioux, part Grizzly."

Their maternal grandfather, Michael Crazysnake, was a Native American activist. In 1970, he was among nearly ninety others who'd staged a year and a half occupation of Alcatraz Island in San Francisco Bay to protest discrimination and to assert Native American rights. Doug and Lenny idolized their grandfather. They had his blessing to work in law enforcement because they had a plan to work on the inside of government while he waged war from the outside.

"Lenny and I are both undercover if you want to know the truth," Doug told me and Wilson when the four of us met at his house for beers late on our first night. "We're learning all we can about the gambling industry because one of these days we will build our own bingo parlors and casinos on our tribal land for the benefit of our people."

"We know the mob will try to infiltrate our operations, so we're putting away as many of them as possible before we open the doors," added Lenny. "We know it is difficult to change things, but it is not impossible."

"I think we can help each other out here, fellas," said Wilson. "Kenda and I want to put away some of these mob guys too. We suspect that the Vegas mob has someone, or maybe a bunch of their people, operating a killer-for-hire service. We have at least four cases, maybe five, in which women were murdered by professionals. In four of them, the unique method used to kill them was the same. We know also that the husbands in each case stood to gain substantially from their wives' deaths."

"And all of those men were regular visitors to Las Vegas and, in particular, the Whitehorse Casino," I added.

I noted that Gio Gamboni was the only known mob guy among the husbands, but the murder of his wife and her lover wasn't done in the same manner as the other four victims.

"Big G is a known player here in Vegas," said Doug Birch. "The local mob gives him respect because he's plugged into the home office in Sicily."

"Gamboni was a regular at the Whitehorse, but word is that he's now in Witness Protection somewhere because he ratted out all the Boston guys under orders from the Sicilians," said Lenny. "I heard some talk around the casino break room that his wife and her boyfriend were taken out. The hit was supposedly ordered from Sicily to repay Big G for clearing out the bad apples in Boston. They didn't give the hit to one of their own because they didn't want it traced to them."

"You mean there is some sort of hit-men-for-hire operation that **they** call?" asked Wilson.

"Well, from what I've heard, it's not like a formal affiliation of dentists or heart specialists. It's more like a loose network of guys who've served with each other, and even against each other. Most of them are military, especially special forces veterans with extensive training and experience. The US and Italian mobs tend to prefer those trained in Europe, the Middle East, and Israel. They fly them in and fly them out, so they aren't easily traced to those who hired them."

"They call these killers 'firemen,' because they extinguish flames, and former flames," Doug added.

Wilson and I found this all very interesting. Maybe Big G and the other four husbands had tapped into the same hit man network even though Gamboni did it through the Sicilians and the other four used mob connections in Vegas.

"So if these husbands all came to Vegas looking to hire a hit man to extinguish their wives, where would they go and who would they talk to in order to make a connection?" I asked.

"You might want to check out a guy named Eugenio Morelli, whose nickname is Smoothie because he thinks of himself as a smooth operator," said Lenny. "He works at the Whitehorse as a pit boss, but he's got a thriving sideline as a fixer who will arrange anything for anyone, as long as it is illegal and there's a big payday in it for him."

"How do we get to him?" I asked.

"Well, I may be able to help you out there, detectives."

"How's that?" Wilson asked.

"Morelli is my boss at the Whitehorse, by day and by night."

"What does that mean?" I asked.

"I'm in charge of security for his pit tables during the day, and, because he likes me so much, he pays me to be his personal bodyguard on some nights when he sets up in the Whitehorse lounge to meet with clients in need of a fixer."

"Holy shit, Lenny! You been holding out on us. Have you ever been there when someone has asked Morelli to connect him to a hit man to kill his wife?"

"Shit, man, that happens every night in Vegas," Lenny joked. "Seriously, Morelli is one of the most cautious mob guys I have ever known. He nearly got burned in an FBI mob bust a few years back, so you can't get anywhere near him when he's meeting with his fixer clients. He makes me stand at least twenty feet away, and I get a thorough pat-down search before and after each shift."

"Have you ever seen him talk to Fred Montgomery?"

"Sure. I've seen them talking in the casino and in the lounge, but I don't know what they discussed. Same with the other husbands you are looking at because their wives were taken out. Most of them are regulars at the Whitehorse, and I've seen them talking to Smoothie, but I can't connect them to any hit men."

"Your task force doesn't have any recording devices in that lounge?" asked Wilson.

"They wish!" said Lenny. "The owners have the entire casino swept for bugs at least twice a day."

"So, how can we get to Morelli?" I asked.

"You might have to stand in line. I know our friends in the FBI are hot to flip him. That's the reason the task force sent me into the Whitehorse. One of my biggest duties is to monitor his activities and look for ways to turn him."

"And?" Wilson said.

"You might have chosen a good time to give it a shot, but you'll have to work with our friends in the Organized Crime Task Force put together by the FBI," said Lenny.

"What do you mean?" Wilson asked.

"Let's set up a meeting with the Bureau's Vegas guy and he can explain it to you."

CHAPTER FIFTEEN

HERR KLEISS

I should send my friend the Captain a thank-you note for serving as a decoy on the Gamboni job. Of course, given that I'm responsible for his limp, he may not be all that happy to hear from me.

The killer of Brandi Gamboni, Kathryn Montgomery, and scores of other women had spotted the Captain just prior to boarding a flight back to Germany at Denver's Stapleton International Airport. After seeing the Captain approaching his gate in the airport terminal, Bruno had pushed to the front of the line rather than risk a messy reunion with the SAS veteran he'd stabbed in Mexico and left for dead.

As his plane departed, Bruno wondered why the

Captain would be in Denver, and then, he made the connection.

My Las Vegas friend had told me that he was arranging a diversion to distract law enforcement from my targets at the resort spa. The Captain must have been my decoy. How perfect! He never would have taken that assignment if he'd known they were using him to help me pull off a hit. And if he saw me in the airport, I'll bet he figures it out just as I did. He will be pissed! Good! He's a righteous asshole.

On this return trip, Bruno's second expertly forged passport from Herr Ernst identified him as Roderick Klein, 30, of Lehre, Germany. Once he was back in his homeland, the professional killer would return to his identity as Bruno Kleiss, an antisocial introvert living with his fierce dogs—two Rottweilers and two Dobermans trained as military guard dogs—on a densely wooded, ninety-acre Bavarian farm outside Garmisch-Partenkirchen.

The farm, which dated back to Roman times, had been purchased from the estate of a Luftwaffe general who spent ten years as a captive of the Soviets before dying of tuberculosis in the farmhouse that Bruno had since renovated. Herr Kleiss, as the locals knew him, kept a half-dozen Brown Swiss dairy cows and four Saanen goats in a bucolic pasture in the shadow of the Zugspitze, Germany's highest peak.

His neighbors grew accustomed to hearing weapons of all kinds being fired on Kleiss's shooting range at one end of his pasture. Given his fondness for guns, and his surly demeanor, they granted Herr Kleiss all the privacy he wanted, even as they speculated about the source of his wealth and the nature of his frequent trips to and from the Munich airport.

MURDEROUS IMPULSES

I mentioned earlier that this was a complex case. It was mind-boggling, really, especially for me as a rookie detective back then. I considered myself street-smart, but this case taught me just how naive I was when it came to the forces that shape a ruthless and cunning bastard like Bruno. Some might argue that, given his background, he was destined to become a serial killer. He was immersed in evil from day one and never benefited from a nurturing parent or grandparent. He was a classic abused kid who became an abuser, a sociopath, and a homicidal maniac, though he had the power to control his worst impulses when on assignment, at least most of the time.

After years of abuse, much of it arranged by his mother or other women, Bruno did not have the same drive as other hormonal boys who wanted to have sex with girls. Bruno wanted to rape, torture, and kill them. Violence was his lust. He had never known a loving relationship of any kind. He only knew brutality. Kindness only raised his suspicion and triggered his paranoia. He trusted no one. To him, a hug was a prelude to pain.

As a result, he learned to strike first and inflict suffering before it was inflicted on him. The only bonds he formed were necessary for self-preservation in a hostile environment. And for him, every environment was hostile. After murdering the nun at Sisters of Saint Mary Angela boardinghouse in Munich, Bruno fled to a bombed-out military base on the outskirts of the city. He had learned in the boardinghouse that a youth gang occupied the base. He presented the gang leaders with items he'd stolen from the nun's room and they gave him shelter.

His first duties were cleaning toilets and taking out garbage, but Bruno quickly moved up in the pecking order, first to drug courier, and then into security and enforcement. When a bigger, stronger, older boy challenged him to a fight after a disagreement,

Bruno gouged out his eyes with a kitchen knife and then threw him in front of a speeding delivery truck. No one challenged him after that.

His reputation for volatility and extreme violence protected him within the gang, and the gang protected him in the streets of Munich. Yet, he realized that if he continued to maim and kill recklessly, he'd become a marked man.

"You should find a legitimate outlet for your violent urges," an older gang leader told him. "Otherwise, either the authorities or your enemies will hunt you down. I'd suggest you join the army. They will train you to kill with even greater skill. Instead of being punished, you will be valued. I have no doubt about that."

Bruno had made many enemies. He'd fought off two attackers on one occasion. On another, he had outrun a pack of four determined to beat him to death. He knew it was only a matter of time before they came after him with more people, or laid in wait and shot him.

As a boy, he'd often heard his mother tell her visitors that she believed his father was a soldier who had trained to compete in the 1944 Winter Olympics before they were canceled because of the war.

"His sport was military patrol," she'd said, which seemed odd to him. He had thought Olympic sports were benign activities like downhill and cross-country skiing, ice skating, hockey, and bobsledding.

Later, Bruno learned that military patrol was a precursor to the biathlon. It began as a competition between military units in each nation and then between units in different nations. Participants were superior athletes who vied in cross-country skiing, mountaineering, and rifle shooting.

"My mother was a whore who lied about everything, so I am not certain if what she said about my father had any truth to it," he told his sergeant. "But this is something I would like to try. I might be good at it."

He proved to be exceptional. His skills as a skier, long-distance runner, boxer, and marksman drew the attention of Lieutenant Colonel Harald Orndorff, a highly decorated officer who was charged with creating the German Army's first special forces unit, Fernspähkompanie 200, which specialized in reconnaissance deep behind enemy lines.

After two years serving in that elite unit, Bruno moved into the federal police force where his military experience in covert activities led to his recruitment into another newly formed elite group, GSG 9, a federal antiterrorist, hostage-rescue, and bomb-disposal unit. He served with them for three years before growing bored.

"All we do is train, train, and train some more. I am tired of shooting at paper targets and straw dummies," he complained.

Corporal Kleiss was not simply itching for action, which is common to most special forces soldiers and law enforcement SWAT team members. Hunting and killing an enemy, terrorists, and criminals was simply a diversion for him. His true obsession was torturing, raping, killing, and dismembering women like those who had tormented him throughout his life.

While serving with GSG 9, Bruno did find a legitimate target that fulfilled his murderous fantasies, but unfortunately, she was arrested before he could get to her. He'd become fixated on West German terrorist Ulrike Marie Meinhof, the former left-wing journalist who was a founding member of the Red Army Faction. The RAF had an unusually large number of female members, which made tracking them down all the more appealing for Corporal Kleiss.

In the spring of 1972, the RAF, known in the press as the "Baader-Meinhof gang," had staged several bombings including a US Army barracks in Frankfurt, a police station in Augsburg, the car of a federal judge, a publishing house in Hamburg, an officers' club in Heidelberg, and another US Army barracks. Ulrike Marie Meinhof was captured in the summer of 1972 when an informant told police where she and another RAF member, Gerhard Muller, were staying.

"We should kill her and all of her terrorist friends," Bruno said to his GSG 9 commander. "If you need someone to do this, please, let me carry it out."

His suggestions were noted by the GSG 9 leadership, but they informed him that Meinhof was in custody and had to be protected until she could stand trial for multiple murder charges.

"One day, you may get your chance, but for now, Corporal, you need to back off," said Lieutenant Colonel Orndorff. "The GSG 9 is a law enforcement unit, you know that. We are not assassins. Too many people—too many politicians, especially— are wary of inviting comparisons to the Nazis. The world condemned Germany for Hitler's savagery. We were defeated and our reputation, not to mention our economy, has suffered as a result. Other nations watch us closely. We must prove that we can be trusted, or we will never be able to rebuild the nation and rejoin the superpowers."

The political pressure only added to Bruno's frustration. He had joined the military and then the elite GSG 9 so that he could kill with impunity, but opportunities to do that had proven to be few and far between, at least from a sociopath's viewpoint.

"GSG 9 was created to stop terrorists, but they won't allow us to kill them," he complained. "Instead, we throw nets over them, gas them, and capture them only to have them escape from prison later. We train constantly on the shooting range and in live-fire exercises, yet we are never authorized to take out real targets. Why, then, must I learn to kill with weapons, with knives, with my fists? Why am I trained to run three miles in under thirty minutes carrying heavy gear and packs? To go to the market?"

Bruno felt he had no other choice than to follow his murderous impulses by exercising his lethal skills unofficially—and illegally. In fact, he had killed repeatedly, but his victims were not military targets or criminals. They were mostly prostitutes, at least a dozen of them throughout Europe. Those kills only temporarily satiated his psychopathic urges. Prostitutes were too easy to kill. There was no real sport in it.

"I have the skills; I want to use them," he said.

Bruno's frustration and dark impulses were shared by others in the GSG 9. He knew more than a few who had left the government's service and become mercenaries, joining veterans of other highly trained military special forces units from around the world.

Their lethal services were contracted on assignment to foreign intelligence agencies wanting to eliminate terrorists, enemies of the state, perceived threats to national security, corrupt politicians, and other threats while maintaining deniability in the international community. Those were the "legitimate" jobs taken by those with at least some moral principles. A wider range of opportunities was open for those driven by money or bloodlust, or—as in Bruno's case—both.

He found more challenging prey when a former special forces comrade told him that he'd become a contract worker for a "network" that paid substantial fees for their specialized skills.

"You only have to take the jobs that appeal to you, and you will make more money than you have ever earned in your life," the friend said. "And, even better, you get to use the training and skills that you have developed through your hard work and sacrifices. But keep in mind, you can't go rogue on these assignments. You must follow the instructions, or you'll never get another call. Do you understand?"

"Yes, please have them contact me," said Bruno.

"I will provide them with your credentials and contact information. You will need a code name that they will use when placing personal ads in the **Sunday Times** to alert you to opportunities suitable for you. What code name do you choose?"

"Gunnar," he said.

PRIVATE CONTRACTOR

Bruno's first contract as "Gunnar Rolf" came a few weeks later. He was amused to see that his contact's code name was Rambo, which was the name of a fictional Vietnam War veteran, a Green Beret, who struggles to adjust to life back home in the US and runs afoul of the law in a novel popular among special forces soldiers and mercenaries.

I doubt that he can live up to the book's character, thought Bruno.

This Rambo turned out to have many similarities

to his fictional namesake, but instead of becoming homeless and hunted by authorities, he was a well-paid mercenary working for drug lords in Southeast Asia. This Rambo recruited Bruno and three other military veterans to provide security for their drug trafficking ring. There also were opportunities to do "bonus jobs" that involved killing rivals, enemies, and other threats to their operation.

Bruno, as Gunnar, made it known that he was available for all the bonus work that they could offer him. And it wasn't long before the offers came.

"Gunnar, I would like you and Thompson to do a bonus job for me," Rambo told him. "There is an informant among our network of heroin transporters and couriers, a boat captain, who has been providing information about our client's operations to an undercover narcotics agent. We want you to take both out."

The plan was to surprise the informant and the federal agent when they met in Laos. Rambo provided both men with submachine guns and silencers as well as latex face masks that made them appear to be Asian.

They were flown to Laos on a private aircraft, which waited for them at a secluded airfield to complete their mission. "I love this work," Gunnar told Thompson as he drove them to the restaurant where the informant and federal agent were meeting.

Thompson took out the fed first. Gunnar was waiting outside the restaurant, knowing the boat captain would try to escape if Thompson hadn't killed him too. The captain ran right into a blast from Gunnar's submachine gun.

The two mercenaries were each paid $50,000.

Bruno was in business.

CHAPTER SIXTEEN

THE FIXER

Eugenio "Smooth Operator" Morelli, known as "Smoothie" for short, was a pit boss on the day shift at the Whitehorse Casino in Las Vegas where he had a dozen table games to monitor including craps, roulette, and poker. His job was to keep everybody happy, except cheaters, thieves, drunks, ass-grabbers, and underage gamblers. Them, he was supposed to keep the hell out.

He monitored the dealers, game supervisors, janitors, players, and anyone else who entered his domain. If there was a dispute involving his crew members and customers, or between customers, he smoothed it out, thus his nickname.

There were eleven other pit bosses, each with

their own domains to monitor. Like Smoothie, each of them also had the more enjoyable task of doling out perks to high rollers, who were valued by the casino because they were big losers. Believe me, if they were consistently big winners, they'd be lucky to get in the door. The perks for high-loss high rollers or "whales" might include "free" meals and cocktails, gambling credits, an extra night or two in a swanky suite, or a hit man to take out a problematic spouse.

Well, that last perk was something that only one pit boss, Smoothie Morelli, could arrange. Smoothie had an off-the-books sideline. By day he was a pit boss. By night he was a fixer who provided services that went beyond anything in his casino job description. He did not do anything illegal because that would put him in danger of losing his permit to work in casinos. However, he did know people who knew people, who might know people who could do illegal things, maybe, depending on who was asking and how much they were paying.

Smoothie was a survivor in the glitzy but treacherous casino environment by being cautious. He did not fix anything directly for anyone, nor did he agree to get things done for people who had not been carefully screened, vetted, and, in some cases, cavity searched by his personal security team, which consisted of Lenny Blackbear, his pit team's security chief who moonlighted as Smoothie's bodyguard when he was in the fixer mode.

Smoothie called Lenny "the Big Chief," but never to his face. Lenny, a large man with fast fists the size of bear paws, had made it clear that he considered such racial stereotypes to be offensive.

The pit boss paid Lenny a hefty sum out of his own pocket when he performed bodyguard duties. He was not aware that Lenny's second salary was augmented by yet a third paycheck from a source unknown to anyone at the Whitehorse Casino. This source was Lenny's primary employer, a federal Organized Crime Task Force, where, as noted earlier, he served in an undercover capacity.

Smoothie trusted Lenny completely, and he valued his menacing presence. No one lingered too long at Smoothie's table when Lenny was hovering nearby. This appealed to Smoothie because it limited opportunities for snitches to record his conversations. Many of Smoothie's childhood friends and associates had been imprisoned thanks to covert recordings made by rats and snitches working for the feds. This was an occupational hazard that he did his best to avoid.

Smoothie was a savvy veteran of the underworld thanks to both nature and nurture. His father, Gianni Morelli, ran a Little Italy restaurant in Chicago that fronted for an illegal gambling operation. Smoothie grew up helping his father with both operations. He called himself "a cook 'n' crook," but only to his best friends from the neighborhood.

Smoothie grew up in Cicero, Illinois, a blue-collar suburb just west of downtown Chicago consisting of hundreds of brick bungalows, churches, taverns, and career criminals. Historically, Cicero was known as a breeding ground for mobsters and their associates. Al Capone moved there early in his career to stay close to the city's unlawful opportunities but just out of reach of the Chicago Police Department.

Cicero is where Smoothie got to know guys who knew guys. There were women there too, of course. Mothers, daughters, grandmothers, aunts, and girlfriends who stayed clear of illegal activities. Women were cast mostly in supporting roles even when they quietly ran the whole shebang.

Being a Cicero native provided Smoothie with street cred as a made guy with moxie, which landed him a high school job as a numbers runner on the South Side. He survived without getting stabbed or shot or arrested, so the mob promoted him to work as a blackjack dealer, and later as a pit boss in his father's backroom operation.

The "Morelli kid" was widely considered to be a mobster prodigy with a bright future on the dark side. Smoothie was crooked, but clean. He avoided booze, drugs, robbing people at gunpoint, and similar vices that destroyed so many other promising Mafia careers. He credited his high school girlfriend and future wife with keeping him on the straight and narrow.

"Peggy would kill me if I did any of that shit," he said fondly.

Margaret "Peggy" Kane had grown up not in Cicero but seven miles to the northwest in the much tonier western suburb of River Forest. She'd met Smoothie at a basketball game between their rival high schools. Four mean-ass Cicero cheerleaders had cornered Peggy, a River Forest cheerleader, outside the girls' restroom. Smoothie happened by and saw an opportunity to be a hero for a hot, rich RFHS girl.

He started to step into the fray, but then stepped

back when Peggy smiled flirtatiously at him and signaled that she had it under control. She was a hot rich girl, true, but Peggy was also the fifth of seven sisters and, therefore, nobody's pushover. Later Smoothie learned that her father, Robert Allen Kane, a Sears corporate executive, was in a sort of Irish mob, which was every bit as tough as the Italian mob, though its members were Notre Dame graduates, more sophisticated in their corrupt ways, and considerably richer.

Smoothie watched in shock and awe as Peggy dispatched the rival cheerleaders who'd confronted her. He felt love bloom in his heart at the sight of the Cicero hellcats beating hasty retreats from a powerful, profane blast of Peggy's Irish fury.

Smoothie was smitten with Peggy's polished-brass personality, not to mention her micromini cheerleader's skirt. Peggy, in turn, thought Smoothie's attempt at chivalry, though lame, was cute, and she liked his dark, handsome features.

"He looks a little like Marlon Brando, if Marlon Brando was really a Sicilian instead of Dutch," she told her fellow cheerleaders.

They dated through their senior years then broke up when Peggy went off to St. Mary's College to major in finance and accounting. Peggy's parents hoped she'd wander across the street from her dormitory and find a nice Notre Dame Law School student to marry, but that didn't happen.

"All those Notre Dame guys care about is football, studying, and drinking until they pass out," she told her parents.

"None of the Notre Dame guys can do it all night like Smoothie," she told her girlfriends. "I'm un-breaking up with him."

Upon Peggy's graduation with honors, Smoothie presented her with a two-carat diamond surrounded by sapphires that he'd bought from his family's fence, Riccardo "ER" Castillo. As a wedding present, Peggy's father gave her a Sears gold credit card that he paid off monthly for the rest of his life.

The wedding was held in the chapel of Holy Name Cathedral in downtown Chicago. The Irish mob and the Italian mob signed a one-day truce for the occasion. One of Mayor Daley's Irish clan members sat on the Kane side. Across the aisle on the Morelli team was his Italian counterpart Tony "Big Shrimp" Marzetti, a member of the Cook County Board and a Mafia capo.

The **Chicago Tribune** sent Ramona Elson, a

cub reporter from the Tempo feature department to cover the high-society wedding, but when she flashed her press credentials, the mob strongman at the cathedral door flashed his Colt semiautomatic pistol and shooed her away. Other than that, there was no wedding drama except for the usual drunken fistfights, one nonlethal stabbing, covert sexual encounters between at least four pairs of groomsmen and bridesmaids, and one Irish-Italian hair-pulling cat fight between rival ex-cheerleaders.

More lethal hostilities broke out in Chicago a few weeks after the Morelli nuptials, but it wasn't the Irish vs. the Italians. This was a war within, an inter-Mafia battle over suburban drug distribution turf between the Northside mob and the Southside mob. Cicero was located at the epicenter of the bloody warfare, which made the newlywed Peggy Morelli nervous, and rightfully so.

"Smoothie, we gotta get outta here!" she said. "There won't be any baby-making for you as long as we are living in a battle zone."

FLIGHT TO FLORIDA

Under threat of a platonic marriage with twin beds, Smoothie agreed to get out of Dodge. He knew exactly where to go to escape the shooting in the streets. South Florida was the established destination of desperation for mobsters on the lam from the law, rival mobsters, their ex-wives, current wives, and the bookies and bankers they'd stiffed.

The **Miami Vice** vibe was a dark reality there long before it was a shiny television show. A sleek yacht parked at the private Caribbean Club marina in Fort Lauderdale served as a symbol of the decadent, coke-snorting, whore-mongering culture that thrived along the Atlantic coast from Pompano Beach to Key West.

The yacht bearing the name **Mutiny on the Booty** was owned by Alfredo "Angel" Evangelista, the Mafia's porn potentate for the East Coast. He was also the silent partner in the Caribbean Club, though the Texas oil man who thought he owned the place was surprised to learn that, just before he accidentally drowned with an anchor around his neck.

Organized crime was rivaled only by organized religion as a corrupting influence in South Florida. Mobsters and their minions ran everything from city governments and police departments to trash collection, bars, restaurants, strip clubs, and boiler rooms pushing bogus municipal-bond and penny-stock scams.

Smoothie Morelli quickly found success in the Swindles, Scams, and Sunshine State, like so many other mid-to-low-echelon criminals who fled to South Florida for similar health reasons.

At Peggy's urging, they'd said so-long to Cicero and moved to the balmy shores of Lauderdale-by-the-Sea. Their first South Florida home was a walk-up apartment above a strip mall with a bikini shop and a mob restaurant below them. Their rear balcony looked out on Highway A1A and offered "just a pinch of ocean view," Peggy told her parents.

"I can walk to the beach and the pier in five minutes," she said. "It's like being on vacation every day."

The only downside was the balcony off their bedroom. They'd dreamed of sitting out there and being lulled to sleep by the crashing of ocean waves. Unfortunately, the balcony hung over the drive-thru lane for a Burger King. If they tried to sit out there, or left the sliding glass doors open, the only thing they could hear was "I'll take a Whopper with cheese, large fries, and a Dr. Pepper. Wait! Make that a diet Dr. Pepper."

"At least it never snows here," she told Smoothie. "And I'll take a drive-thru over a drive-by anytime."

Members of rival Mafia families were less likely

to shoot each other in South Florida than in New York City, Detroit, or Chicago. Turf wars were rare.

"It's more like the Wild West down here. There's plenty of graft for everyone," Smoothie's new boss told him.

Technically, Smoothie's move to Florida was a job transfer. He walked right into a new Mafia post as a pit boss for a high-stakes card casino that was gambling's version of a movable feast.

To avoid drawing attention from law enforcement, the unlicensed and untaxed casino nights were held one week in a Fort Lauderdale finger isle mansion, the next in a Sunrise condo, the next in a Plantation ranch house or a Hallandale nursing home rec room. The gaming ring was run by a horse racing capo from the same Chicago crime family that secretly owned the Whitehorse Casino in Vegas. He'd had to relocate due to an investigation of doping—both horses and humans—in his Arlington Park racing stable.

In fact, the two very different but lucrative mob gambling endeavors shared an equine theme. The South Florida operation was headquartered in a Tamarac Thoroughbred training stable. The saddle-free tack room served as a conference center for planning and strategy meetings. A few of the lower-echelon employees, Haitian immigrants who were the moving men and truck drivers, lived in stalls next to the only actual four-legged residents, Snort and Bugs.

Snort was an eighteen-year-old Thoroughbred. Bugs was genetically a mule, but the city-slicker mobsters didn't know the difference.

"That one named Bugs has really long ears for a Thoroughbred, don't you think?" said Smoothie, who had been called to the stable to meet with the ring's local leader on his day off.

"Don't say anything derogatory because that horse can hear every word," joked his boss, Mickey Spagnullo Jr. "Okay, let's get down to business, Smoothie. I called you in here today because you've done good as a pit boss even though we move the whole damn show every couple days. We've kept an eye on you, and we have all been impressed. You run a clean game. You've also spotted a bunch of card cheats, and we appreciate that too."

"Aw, thanks, boss. That's a relief. I thought you called me in to bust my balls for something," Smoothie said.

"Naw, in fact, you've done so well we're promotin'

you to the main office, the Whitehorse Casino in Vegas," Spagnullo said. "They put out a call for some new blood because a few of their pit bosses developed sticky fingers and we had to cut them off—their fingers, that is."

"Well, you know I'm a straight arrow, boss. I never had so much as a parking ticket."

"Yep, we know that, too, which is good because you can't work in a Vegas casino if you have any criminal convictions on your record. You're just the kinda guy they are looking for. So, we'll cover all your moving expenses. I know you are gonna miss your Burger King buddies and the beach, but, believe me, you will earn a lot more in Vegas, so you can afford a much nicer place. Maybe with a balcony over a Red Lobster or an International House of Pancakes. That would be a step up, right?"

It proved to be a fortuitous move for Smoothie. Just three months after he was promoted to the Whitehorse, the FBI swarmed all over the South Florida gambling ring, busted a dozen of the mob crew and ten customers, including two state representatives, a mayor, a priest, and a police chief.

The Thoroughbred, Snort, and the mule, Bugs,

were donated to the Broward County Sheriff's Youth Ranch, but not before Bugs was given a commendation and an extra scoop of oats coated in molasses for public service. The award was from the FBI's Fort Lauderdale chief, Dave Wieczorek.

"Ol' Bugs brought down the whole operation thanks to that listening device we put in its halter!" the fed said.

Now, in truth, Peggy was not all that happy with the move to Vegas.

"It's like the desert, with more traffic," she said.

She complained less when Smoothie began bringing home $10,000 a week from his job as pit boss at the Whitehorse Casino and another $20,000 a week from his sideline as a fixer. No more tiny apartments for the Morelli family. They moved into a four-bedroom split level with a pool and spa in suburban Henderson, Nevada.

"Baby, now we can get serious about starting a family," Smoothie said after moving in.

"Oh, honey, I been meaning to tell you something about that," Peggy said coyly.

"What?"

"Sweetie, I am finally pregnant! And it's twins!"

"Twins! Holy moly! That's terrific! Let's celebrate!

Can we still do it? It's a special occasion, so I wanna try a new position in the spa!"

Smoothie and his wife would look back on those early Vegas years as the best of times.

Unfortunately for them, the times were a changing.

CHAPTER SEVENTEEN

JOINING FORCES

"How do you feel about working with a disorganized grime trash farce?" Wilson asked me on the way to a meeting at the FBI office in Las Vegas.

"That's your nickname for the Organized Crime Task Force?" I asked. "I've never worked with one. Are they that bad?"

At that point in my law enforcement career, I had not had the pleasure, or displeasure, of participating in a law enforcement group grope. I would work with several of them over the years, but this first experience would prove to be enlightening—and very nearly a disaster.

Combined task forces bring together a team from local, state, and federal law enforcement. They are formed to investigate criminal activities that cross local and state boundaries such as drug and sex trafficking, street gangs, pornography, and organized crime.

Few of these operations combining investigators from multiple jurisdictions are without turbulence, but over the years even those that have had conflicts eventually nabbed the likes of the Unabomber, the Golden State Killer, and the DC Sniper.

"I've been involved in these federal task forces a couple times, and they are just a nightmare to manage," Wilson said. "The leaders have to be really strong and well-organized, or the operation can turn into shitstorms in a flash," he added. "Too often, the worst of human nature prevails. It's like herding bobcats because the participants are mostly bull-headed guys, each with their own ideas about how things should be done."

Boys will be boys in any group of men thrown together from different organizations for a special purpose.

"When you get all of these people from different law enforcement agencies and backgrounds together in a task force, it can easily become a clusterfuck,"

Wilson continued. "Egos clash. Turf wars are waged. Everybody wants credit. Nobody takes responsibility. Old rivalries and grudges kick in. I've never been involved in a multiagency investigation that ended with me feeling, 'Well, that was just a wonderful experience.'"

I just nodded my head, playing the rookie role, letting the senior detective pour his knowledge into my skull.

"Many heads are better than one," I said, lamely tossing in my two cents.

"I hope you are right, rookie," he replied.

G-MEN

Wilson and I liked the Vegas Vice cop Doug Birch and his brother, Lenny, the undercover fed. They were good people. Still, we were wary of working with big unwieldy groups like the Organized Crime Task Force, especially the FBI and their newest generation of agents, who tended to be less polished and more undisciplined than the senior agents. Their veteran street guys, the special agents trained as criminal investigators, were usually first-rate. Most were military veterans, and many had degrees in law or forensic accounting.

"The only feds that I've had problems with are the youngest generation. Most of them are cocky frat boys who have never had to dig through a dumpster," Wilson said.

"Usually, it's not the agents who frost my shorts, it's the bureaucrats above them. They are political weasels beholding to some elected asshole in DC," he continued.

Wilson had a point. Our police chief had to answer to the mayor and the city council, too, but the political pressure from them was nothing compared to what comes down on the FBI and any federal task force. They are controlled by power players and bureaucrats in Washington, DC, all of whom have their own games going.

"The FBI bureaucrats act like everything they do is a top secret big hairy deal, mostly because it makes them feel important," Wilson said. "I worked one joint investigation in which the FBI guys refused to give me a copy of one of their five-oh-twos, which is their fancy-ass name for an investigation report. We had to have all these damned meetings before they finally agreed to hand over a copy of 'some portions' of their report, but for some damned reason they decided I shouldn't be able to read the page numbers. They had an agent block them out when he copied each page."

"Jesus, that makes no sense," I said.

"Well, apparently they didn't want me to know what section of the report the pages came from, or some bullshit like that," Wilson said. "But get this, the dumbass FBI bureaucrat doing the redacting blocked out the wrong side of each page, so I could see the page numbers anyway. When I told them I made multiple copies and sent them out to other agencies, they had a stroke! Of course, I didn't really do that, I was just fucking with the idiots."

Colorado Springs had a big FBI office, as many as twenty-two agents at one time over the years, because they had jurisdiction over four military bases there, including the US Air Force Academy, Cheyenne Mountain Air Force Stations, Fort Carson Army Post, and Schriever Air Force Base. All were on federal land and a lot of it. Fort Carson alone covers more than 130,000 acres, all property of the US government.

So our police department, and county and state law enforcement, deferred to their military police and the FBI on criminal matters there.

"Oh Lord, I had one of those cases of an army

corporal killing his girlfriend in Colorado Springs, and the FBI sent one of their eager-beaver, newly badged, full-of-himself shitheads to meet with me," Wilson recalled. "He came in his Brooks Brothers suit, leaned over my desk, stuck out his hand, and said, 'I'm Special Agent Edwin Stevenson the fourth.'

"I just looked up and said, 'Well, what is so fucking special about you?' Then I told him my favorite FBI joke."

"You mean the one about . . . ?"

Wilson could not be stopped.

"I went to a law enforcement K-9 demonstration the other day. They had a local bomb squad dog, a DEA drug-sniffing dog, and an FBI attack dog. The bomb squad K-9 went first. It ran onto an airplane and three seconds later came out with a bomb in its mouth. Next up was the DEA dog. They sent it into a house and it did a quick search and found a package of cocaine. And, finally, they unleashed the FBI dog, and guess what it did?"

"I'll bite," I said with a sigh.

"The FBI dog fucked the other two K-9s and then called a press conference!"

Wilson had told me that joke at least a dozen

times, and at least one of us always got a big kick
out of it.

RIPE FOR FLIPPING

The FBI's special agent assigned to the Organized
Crime Task Force in Las Vegas was Christopher
Shawn. We got along with him because he had actually paid his dues, unlike a lot of the Bureau's frat
boys. His first job after earning a college degree in
criminal justice was working security on a Mississippi River gambling boat secretly owned by the
Chicago mob. He spent three years throwing card
counters, poker cheats, and slots scammers into the
Big Muddy. When he realized his real bosses were
mobsters, he exchanged his testimony against them
for a job with the Bureau.

The FBI agent in charge of hiring said Shawn's
job application stood out for its originality. "Look,
I was young and naive. I thought the rich downstate
restaurant guy really owned the riverboat. What did
I know? My goal has always been to be an FBI agent,
so let's make a deal."

For his penance, Shawn had to go undercover
for five years as a Hells Angels motorcycle gang
member in Oakland, California. Then the FBI

gave him another five years working undercover in a long-term investigation of organized crime operations in Baltimore, Detroit, Birmingham, and El Paso, Texas.

"So, gentlemen, this is not my first rodeo," he said to Wilson and me to open the meeting arranged by the Birch brothers.

"I was just admiring your ostrich-skin boots. Nice!" said Wilson, a master of cow-bromances.

We explained our interest in Smoothie Morelli as someone who might lead us to the hit men we suspected of killing Kathryn Montgomery, Brandi Gamboni, and the other known members of the dead wives' club from Seattle, San Diego, and Salt Lake City.

"Based on what Lenny here has told us about Smoothie's activities as a fixer, we think he may have connected the husbands of those victims to the same network of professional hit men in Europe hired by the mob when they don't want to use their own people," Wilson explained.

"Do you have any proof of a connection between Smoothie and the husbands?" Agent Shawn asked.

"Yes," said Lenny, jumping in on our behalf. "They've shown me photographs of each of them. Some

I remembered because they are regular customers at the Whitehorse. Others I recognized from their meetings with Smoothie in the lounge, and a few I found by matching the dates of their flights to Vegas with our surveillance videos from the casino. Other than Big G Gamboni, who may have used his own mob connections to contact the network, all the husbands on your list have been in the Whitehorse, which means each of them had access to Smoothie and his fixer services."

Shawn put his thousand-dollar boots up on his desk, obviously man-flirting with Wilson. I figured it wouldn't be long before they were swapping John Wayne quotes over brewskis.

"Well, detectives, your timing is fortuitous for a couple reasons," he said. "Thanks to your task force friend, Lenny, we now have a truckload of incriminating shit that we can use to haul in Smoothie so we can pressure him to flip on his fellow Mafiosos. In addition, Agent Birch here has learned that after years of trying, Smoothie and his beloved wife finally found the glorious path to fertility, and she recently gave birth to twins."

"That's just peachy, I'm happy for them. I may even send a congratulatory flower basket, but what has that got to do with our investigation?" I asked.

"Excellent question, Detective Cranky," said Agent Shawn. "Should I explain, or do you want to run and get a biscuit first to ease your sullen mood?"

"Sorry, I haven't slept much because our hotel is really a whore house and everyone else on our floor spends the night banging like banshees," I said.

"No problem," said Agent Shawn. "They do call it Sin City for a reason. But to answer your question, Lenny tells me that Smoothie may be the boss of his pit and a rising star in the mob hierarchy, but his tough Irish wife rules the roost at home. She has two screaming babies now, and she is withholding marital bliss from Smoothie until he figures out a way to leave the mob and get them safely the hell out of Vegas."

"And you can make that happen?" Wilson asked.

"It will go like this, Kemosabe," said Lenny. "We'll offer the lovely Morelli family a safe haven and a cozy new life in the federal Witness Protection Program in exchange for Smoothie's cooperation in your investigation and ours. If he helps the Bureau bring down the hit man Big G hired to kill his wife, that will clear out a space in the program for his family. Nice and tidy, right?"

"Terrific, so, what's our next move?" I asked.

"How are you planning to present all of this to Smoothie without tipping off his mob associates?"

"Detective Kenda, did you ever play doctor as a kid?"

CHAPTER EIGHTEEN

PUTTING THE SQUEEZE ON SMOOTHIE

Peggy Morelli arrived as scheduled at the pediatrician's office with her twins, Jessica and Daniella. Her husband, and the twins' proud father, Whitehorse pit boss and mob fixer Eugenio "Smoothie" Morelli, gladly accompanied them.

"Please take your seats in Examining Room Number Three; Dr. Rossi will be right in to see you," the nurse said.

The Morelli parents settled into two chairs, each holding one of the twins.

"Hey, baby, you wanna take the kids to the park after this?" asked Smoothie. "I've got the rest of the day off."

"That would be nice, honey, but they are due for

their shots and I'm afraid they won't be in the mood for the park," Peggy replied.

"What shots? Aren't they too young to get stuck with needles?"

"The nurse said that the six-month visit includes shots for diphtheria, tetanus, and pertussis."

"Are you kidding me? That's crazy! I don't think I can stand to watch them stick our tiny little girls three times and inject them with all that shit."

"Oh, Smoothie, it's not three shots. They combine it all in one, so it won't be that bad. I hope."

Just then, there was a polite knock on the examining room door, and in walked a fit-looking man in a suit and dress cowboy boots.

"Hey, buddy, I think you have the wrong room or something," said Smoothie.

"Good morning, Mr. Morelli. Dr. Rossi will be meeting with your wife and children in another room shortly. I'm Special Agent Christopher Shawn of the FBI's Organized Crime Task Force, and I want to discuss with you some matters of great importance to your family's future," he said.

The stunned couple had no response at first. Both wrapped their arms around their daughters as if this G-man had threatened to make them wards of the state.

Peggy choked back tears. Eugenio's fight or flight impulse kicked in, but he was pinned to the chair by Daniella, who was already up nine pounds from her birth weight.

Agent Shawn continued with the polished charm of a Mercedes salesman. "First of all, let me congratulate you on your two beautiful daughters. I have two daughters myself, and I know you are in for some wonderful times. I also know these six-month shots can be hard on them, so you might be in for a long night or two."

Peggy fired off an Irish death stare at Agent Shawn, and then at Smoothie, but neither knew what to say to the FBI agent with the demented grin. Wilson and I were watching on a security camera in Dr. Rossi's office, and Agent Shawn was playing it exactly according to the plan we'd dreamed up in a bar-table brainstorming session a couple weeks earlier.

CULLING THE HERD

There was nothing fancy about our scheme. Predators have been culling the weakest prey from the herd since the age of the dinosaurs. Organized crime families are a particularly unruly pack, consisting of paranoid, volatile, and violent individuals, so isolating their members has long been an effective tactic for law enforcement.

The mob, like other, more innocent fraternities, holds sophisticated ceremonies to impress upon its members that they are part of an elite brotherhood reliant on a mutual trust. Honoring the code of silence is crucial to maintaining those bonds.

It is all bullshit, of course. There is no honor among thieves, drug dealers, sex traffickers, and their slithering ilk. They'd stab their own mothers to get the family jewels. But the mob dons and capos put up the facade of honor to protect themselves and the millions they leech from society.

They strictly enforce their code of silence when it is breeched because one well-connected "rat" can take down the entire fragile organization. The mob makes a big show of punishing informants, or suspected informants. They want the message to be clear. **Turn on us, and you will die a thousand deaths**.

As a result, Mafia members and their minions are governed by fear more than loyalty, which makes crime families vulnerable to divide-and-conquer strategies. Each conniving member can be trusted only to put his own interests first. Given the opportunity to rat out their cronies for self-enrichment or self-preservation, they will flee the herd without looking back.

Our goal, then, was to wrangle Smoothie Morelli away by tossing a noose around his neck.

"We'll offer him and his family protection for the rest of their lives if he cooperates," said Agent Shawn. "And we'll offer to feed him to the wolves if he doesn't."

The US Witness Protection Program was created to give safe passage to rats and their families, among others. It has been a useful if expensive tool, but even so, flipping a member of the mob requires a delicate touch. I'm proud to say that my mentor, Detective Wilson, and our coconspirators, devised a doozy of a plan to make Eugenio Morelli sing like a sell-out soprano.

Lenny Birch provided a key bit of information to help us set the trap.

"Smoothie plays the hard ass as a pit boss, and he's a good one. He's also tough as hell when working as a mob fixer," the undercover fed explained. "He is as cold and as ruthless as they come when he is working, but when he heads home to the wife and kids, he becomes Ward fucking Cleaver. I kid you not!"

"Who? Oh, you're talking about the father of Beaver and Wally on **Leave It to Beaver**? I was more into **Father Knows Best.** I watched the reruns every day after school," Agent Shawn said. "Betty was so hot."

Lenny ignored the younger FBI agent and explained that, unlike most mob reprobates, Smoothie was a loyal husband and doting father. He didn't screw around on his wife, not even with the hookers who trolled the casino day and night.

"He really is a family guy, believe it or not, and after years of trying to make babies, he was over the moon when Peggy had the twins," Lenny said. "I have no doubt that he could order up two or three hits in one night and then go home and read Dr. Seuss bedtime stories to his kids."

Morelli's devotion to family included taking days off to help the missus when the twins have a doctor's appointment.

"So, that could be our chance to get Smoothie alone and play Let's Make a Deal," Lenny said. "We'll get their pediatrician to cooperate and send Agent Shawn here into the examining room to bedazzle Morelli with his Rhinestone Cowboy bullshit.

Even if the mob has a tail on Smoothie, they'll never know what happened in that examining room, right? Doctor-patient privilege? What do they call it, the Hippocritic oath or something like that?"

"I think that's the **Hippocratic** oath, but yeah, you're right. Good plan," said his brother, Doug.

Agent Shawn and officials with the federal Witness Protection Program worked out the package deal for Morelli to win his cooperation with our investigation. The Bureau was all in because they shared our belief that the same guy, or at least the same network of guys, who killed Mrs. Montgomery, also took out Brandi Gamboni and the other three victims in San Diego, Seattle, and Salt Lake City.

PLAYING DOCTOR

Our trap was baited and set, and Smoothie walked right into it at the pediatrician's office. Once Agent Shawn had introduced himself to the family, he called the nurse back into the examining room to clear out the wife and kids.

"Mrs. Morelli, Dr. Rossi will see you and the twins in Room Number Five, while your husband and this gentleman continue their discussion. Here, let me take Daniella off your hands, Mr. Morelli."

Once Peggy and twins were out of the room, Agent Shawn turned off the charm and cranked up the heat. Just like we'd planned, Agent Shawn would claim to have more damning evidence on Smoothie than truly existed. There is no law that says we can't lie to criminals during an investigation, so, yeah, it happens all the time. Tough shit. We were dealing with mobsters, not soccer moms.

"Mr. Morelli, I am here to offer you a safer and more secure life for you and your family. I know that is something you and your wife want. I also know that you have been looking for a way to put your life of crime and your mob associates behind you. I'm here today to show you that path to a new life. Please, just listen as I lay it out for you."

Smoothie could not have interrupted even if he wanted to. His throat had turned to a dry gully and his brain was scrambled by thoughts of his imminent doom.

I am so dead, he thought.

Agent Shawn observed that the blood had drained from Morelli's face. He was glad there was a doctor nearby just in case the scumbag went down with a heart attack.

"First of all, you should know that we have been

monitoring your activities at the Whitehorse and around town for quite some time now," Agent Shawn said. "We have a mountain of evidence, showing your involvement in illegal activities and your association with known members of the mob.

"Let me lay out a hypothetical scenario for you. Let's say that our evidence includes many hours of videos and recordings of your meetings with at least four men whose wives were subsequently murdered—and all those women were killed in re-markably similar ways. This has led us to believe that all four women were shot to death by the same individual, a professional hit man.

"Or is that just one hell of a coincidence, Mr. Morelli?"

The mobster could only shake his head, but the of-fensive noises coming from his stomach spoke volumes.

"We do not think this is a coincidence at all, Mr. Morelli, because none of these four men have crim-inal records. None of them are licensed gun owners. We do not believe any of them would have enough balls to shoot a pigeon, let alone their wives.

"So, tell me this, Mr. Morelli. How hard do you think the FBI would have to squeeze their nuts to get one, or all of them, to give you up as the guy who connected them to the hired killer who took out their wives?"

A faint whimper escaped from Smoothie's bloodless lips.

"Let me continue the scenario for you," Shawn said. "Once we had reasonable cause to arrest your ass, we would make sure to do it at the Whitehorse Casino. We would parade you on a perp walk to end all perp walks. Television, radio, newspapers. The whole media circus. Lights, camera, action. The headlines would read: **Mob Boss Nailed in Whitehorse Casino for Operating Murder-for-Hire Scheme**. I'm betting that prick Mike Wallace and **60 Minutes** will be all over this. He'll probably take his camera crew into your father's restaurant to interview your poor parents. And what the hell will your Mick father-in-law say? Just for starters, he'll send Peggy and the kids to some Irish safe house and then he'll send the entire Irish Republican Army to stomp on your head."

Shawn read the panicked look on Smoothie's face and moved in for the kill.

"We know you are just a mob grunt, of course, but the real bosses in Vegas and Chicago will not be happy with the bad publicity generated by your arrest for your side scam. They don't like that kind of attention, do they? Once we lock you up in prison, they will send the slice-and-dice teams after you. That is where you will die. You will never see your beautiful little girls go off to their first day of school or walk down the aisle in their weddings. Your grandchildren will grow up never having known you."

Agent Shawn paused to let the scenario sink in.

Eugenio Morelli put his face in his hands and sobbed.

"What do you want from me?" he asked.

His voice was muffled because his hands were still over his face.

"All you have to do is give up your hit man, the guy who specializes in killing rich housewives, and we'll put you in the Witness Protection Program where you, Mrs. Morelli, and the twins will live happily ever after.

"Or you can die in jail next week because the mob will figure you for a snitch and kill your sorry ass before you can give us any more information."

THE FLIPPED FIXER

The Morelli twins went home that day with a clean bill of health but sore thighs and slightly elevated temperatures. Their daddy went home with a deal he could not refuse. Smoothie was locked into a life-or-death decision, neatly packaged and presented by our mini–task force.

The next day Smoothie returned to his job as pit boss at the Whitehorse Casino, and that night, he took his usual seat in the lounge to work his side gig as a mob fixer. We didn't put a wire on him because we didn't have to.

Every night when he went home, the FBI had two agents waiting to debrief him not just on the day's events, but also on his methods for connecting clients like our suspect Fred Montgomery to hired killers.

"How do guys like Fred Montgomery find you?"

"Bartenders, waitresses, hookers, cab drivers; I pay them all for keeping their ears open and sending clients my way," Morelli said. "They don't send them to me directly, of course. They are screened by a bunch of my people who vet them before I'll talk to them. We weed out the pissed-off drunks, idiots who can't keep their mouths shut, and anyone who doesn't have the dough to pay for the services we provide. And, of course, we are always watching out for undercover douchebags like you guys have out there."

Agent Shawn let that slide. Smoothie still had no idea that his favorite personal bodyguard, Lenny Blackbear, was a federal undercover agent.

"So did you meet with Fred Montgomery once he cleared all of your super-duper security walls?"

"Yeah, we met in his room at the Flamingo around three in the morning," Morelli said. "I knew him as a whale at our place. He was a regular. He dropped a lot of money at the Whitehorse over the years. We rewarded him with free drinks, free meals, a big line of credit, and, on special occasions, two or three hookers to take home for dessert."

"Funny how the big losers feel like winners when you hand them a few freebies, even after they've lost hundreds or thousands of dollars," said Agent Shawn.

"Sure as hell, you've got that right," Smoothie said. "Casinos take suckers like Fred Montgomery to the bank!"

In their banter, Smoothie himself was being played like a sucker by the FBI agent, but it never occurred to him.

"What did Fred Montgomery say about needing to have his wife killed?"

"Same old story that I hear all the time. He said she was a rich bitch who'd never worked a day in her life and that she'd cut him off from all the dough she'd inherited," Smoothie said. "He claimed she'd left him no choice when she shut down access to her account."

"What did he say, exactly?"

"Something like, 'She wants me to get down on my knees and beg, but that's not happening. I'm sick of her lording it over me. I want her dead and I'll pay whatever it takes to make it happen, so I never have to worry about money again.'"

SMOOTHIE'S OPERATION

Once we guaranteed the safety of his family, Morelli gushed like a fire hose that we couldn't shut off if we wanted to.

"Getting rich women killed wasn't really a big part of my services, you gotta understand that," he claimed. "I mean, I did it when someone was willing to pay big bucks, but most of the time people came to me to have one of our enforcers break a guy's arm because he wouldn't pay back a loan, or they'd want me to use some mob clout to get a lawyer or a reporter to back off."

Morelli considered himself a problem solver, and, basically, that's what he was. Except some of the problems he solved ended up dead.

"Smoothie, you probably could have made a legit fortune as a Hollywood talent agent or some kind of crisis-management specialist," said Agent Shawn during one of their nightly sessions. "Now, tell us about the guy who killed Fred Montgomery's wife. Who is he, and how did you find him?"

"Hell, I didn't know his name. I never wanted to know his name. Are you crazy?"

"Well then, how did you connect him and Fred Montgomery?"

"It was all done through intermediaries. Nobody knew nobody's name. Nobody wanted to know nobody's name."

"Who was the first guy you called to make this happen for Montgomery?"

"One of the mob guys has a contact in the Cosa Nostra in Sicily who was an ex-military guy, some sort of special forces," Morelli said. "The ex-soldier had been a mercenary and then worked for private security companies all over the world. He knows a lot of other former military types around Europe with special training who are addicted to that lifestyle. They crave action. Some of the crazier ones crave killing, and they work as hit men under contract. The mob dons and capos use them when they want someone taken out but they don't want it traced back to them."

"Sounds like an international version of Murder Inc., or Serial Killers Anonymous," Agent Shawn said. "How do you make the first connection? You still haven't told me that, and we have a deal, Smoothie."

"I have a guy who calls a guy in London."

"And? You are trying my patience here. You don't want to take a perp walk down the Vegas Strip, do you?"

"I'm not trying to avoid answering the question, it's just a secretive and complicated fucking process," Smoothie said.

The FBI agent was getting frustrated with the runaround.

"So, what do you tell the mob guy you call to tell the guy in London to tell the frickin' hit man, Smoothie?"

"I just tell the mob guy that I have a job for a hitter. Then he notifies the guy in London who places a personal ad in London's biggest weekend newspaper, the **Sunday Times**, with a special code that he and the hitter have worked out. Then, the hitter calls the London connection who lays out the basic time and location of the hit. The hit man then decides whether he is interested. If he gives the green light, the London guy gives him an untraceable number to call. It's a special number that bounces all over hell but eventually rings on my phone, and we seal the deal without exchanging names or birthday cards. We agree on a fee, and I wire the money to the mob guy who takes a cut and wires it to the London guy who takes a cut and then he takes cash to a designated drop, usually a locker in an airport or train station somewhere . . . I told you it was fucking complicated!"

"What's the going rate for having a rich wife killed these days, Smoothie?"

"Well, this guy is a real pro, and the target was extremely wealthy, and there was travel involved . . ."

"Fuck, just answer the damned question, Smoothie. How much was he paid?"

"Mr. Montgomery paid a hundred fifty thousand, so by the time everyone, including me, took a cut, I suppose the actual shooter got a hundred grand or so."

"Jesus, that's a good paycheck."

"Yeah, that's top rate," Smoothie said. "I could probably find you ten guys hanging out at the Whitehorse who'd do it for a hundred bucks, but then, they'd probably fuck it up, or rat me out to the feds if someone looked at them cross-eyed."

"Getting back to Mrs. Montgomery's killer, how did you get her location and other information to the hit man?" Agent Shawn asked.

"I sent a packet with her photos, addresses, phone numbers, routines, and all that shit to a courier service in Munich. They have a will-call desk where he picked it up."

"Who do you address the packet to in this case?"

"Gunnar Rolf, but I'm sure that's not his real name. My guess is that nobody knows this guy's real name. He's probably had so many fake names, he can't remember what it says on his real birth certificate."

CHAPTER NINETEEN

BAIT & SWITCH

The next mob client referral for the hit man code-named Gunnar Rolf would come to him from Eugenio "Smoothie" Morelli, courtesy of the Federal Bureau of Investigation, according to our carefully concocted plan.

Special Agent Shawn laid it out for Morelli.

"I want you to have your mob guy's Cosa Nostra connection place a personal ad in the **Sunday Times** for your pal Gunnar. This is what it should say: Gunnar Rolf: You are the one and only one for me. I am here to pleasure you. Please call Lisa.

"When he responds, make the deal. Just pay him whatever he usually gets. We'll provide the cash. If he balks at coming back to Colorado, throw in another twenty grand. Once he's signed on, send him this packet of information, which includes the name of the client hiring him."

The "client" identified in the packet was the fictional Rogan "Lefty" O'Rourke, and the target was his fictional wife, Amelia. The information packet said O'Rourke would be playing in a pro-am charity golf tournament set for the weekend of October 18–19 at the Rocky Waters Golf & Ski Resort in Vail, just a couple weeks before the end of their golf season.

If this had been a real wife hit instead of an FBI-sponsored charade set up to capture or kill Gunnar, O'Rourke's golf partners would have provided his alibi.

"We have to make it look like a clean deal to protect the husband like the other hits on rich wives, otherwise Gunnar will smell a rat," said Agent Shawn. "This is costing the Bureau a bundle. Shutting down half of a golf resort ain't cheap, even with a government discount in the off-season. If we screw this up, I may have to become a hit-man-for-hire myself."

The Rocky Waters Golf & Ski Resort, the scene for the setup, was situated on more than two thousand acres in Hanover Valley, seven miles outside the city of Vail. There were two villages featuring hotels, restaurants, and shops on the property that had a base elevation of 8,200 feet and a summit elevation of 11,500 feet.

Galena Mines Village was the destination setup for downhill and cross-country skiing, ice skating, and other cold-weather sports. Tucked next to it was Eagles Nest Village, which encompassed two eighteen-hole championship golf courses—Rooks Creek Run and Vermilion Valley—as well as horseback, bicycle, and hiking trails; an Olympic swimming pool and water park; basketball courts; and facilities for other warm-weather activities.

The Bureau had arranged to take over the gated northern half of Eagles Nest Village, where the Rooks Creek Run golf courses ran alongside the lower elevation portions of the Galena Mines ski runs.

"That area is fairly isolated from the rest of the resort so we can shut it down for the weekend, minimizing any risk of innocents being injured or killed by stray bullets if the suspect puts up a fight rather than surrendering," said Agent Shawn on a call to Wilson and me. "We've planned for every contingency. We even brought in an FBI chopper that will be manned by sharpshooters. We're hoping this Gunnar doesn't decide to commit suicide by law enforcement. Either way, in a car or a casket, he's not leaving that mountain without an FBI escort."

Shawn said the Bureau would stage the golf tournament with all the usual fanfare for Gunnar's benefit.

"We want this to look like a legit pro-am tournament because we're fairly certain that he, or his accomplices, will do surveillance prior to the day of the planned hit on the fake O'Rourke's fake wife," the FBI agent said. "We've hired a golf event company to set it all up like the real thing, but the golfers, both pro and am, and even the caddies, will be FBI SWAT team members from across the country. None of them are professional-level golfers, but all will be expert marksmen. Everyone will be armed. Each golf bag will contain the usual irons, clubs, and putters, as well as a small arsenal of semiautomatic and automatic weapons. Even the cart girls are FBI agents who can make beergaritas and handle a submachine gun."

"I'm not a golfer and I couldn't afford to play these courses even if I was, but I have a question about your plan," I said.

"Yes, Detective Kenda."

"Do people really golf up in the mountains this time of year?" I asked. "Isn't October up there too cold for these assholes in their golf shorts and short-sleeve shirts?"

"Good question, but actually, the real golf pro at Rocky Waters, John Lumley, said it is the best time of year for playing their courses because of the fall colors and cooler temperatures," Shawn said. "But then, maybe he told us that so he could charge the Bureau more for shutting down his operation for the weekend."

"Okay, if that's what the golf pro says, it must be true," I said. "Let's just hope Gunnar isn't a golf fan who figures out in five seconds that your SWAT team members can't keep the ball on the fairway."

"We thought about that, so to make them look more authentic, we are issuing them really ugly golf shirts and pants in wild colors with bad patterns and plaids," joked Shawn.

"That should do it!" I said.

The FBI agent walked us through the plan for "G-Day" at the resort.

The packet sent to Gunnar laid it all out for the hit man. It said O'Rourke and his wife would be staying in a suite on the top floor of the Osprey Lodge, which was a three-story, high-end, four-star hotel tucked into the mountainside. It was the most isolated location, situated between a ski run and a fairway between the ski resort and the golf resort.

Our plan, as relayed to Gunnar, was that O'Rourke would tell his wife that he had a 7:30 a.m. tee time, but he would arrange for a waiter to bring her breakfast in bed two hours later, while he was on the golf course. Gunnar was to knock on her door at 9:30 a.m., posing as a waiter with a food cart. Once the wife let him into the room, he was to kill her and then get out. O'Rourke would return after playing his round and then having lunch and a few drinks with his partners, only to discover his murdered wife.

That was the clean in-and-out scenario created for Gunnar.

"We want him to think this is easy pickings, a relaxed golf resort without much, if any, serious security, allowing for a quick hit on an unsuspecting female victim in her hotel room. All of this would unfold during a golf tournament packed with participants and spectators who wouldn't pay attention to another guy in a golf cap," Agent Shawn said.

"That's what he'll be thinking. In reality, the scenario will not be so accommodating for this serial wife killer," he added.

The FBI's plan was to trap Gunnar in the hotel hallway, swarming him from all sides with heavily armed, body-armored SWAT members as soon as he reached the locked door to the O'Rourke suite in the middle of the hotel's top floor. There would be no Mrs. O'Rourke waiting for her breakfast-in-bed service. The room would be locked and unoccupied.

The SWAT members would pour out of every room on the floor, cutting off all exits and overwhelming Gunnar, forcing him to surrender. Once the hit man was secured, the FBI planned to transport him by helicopter to the maximum security federal prison near Florence, Colorado, about 140 miles to the southeast.

"Upon his arrest, we will issue warrants for Fred Montgomery and the three other husbands known to have secured Gunnar's services through Smoothie and his Mafia-run murder-for-hire operation," said Agent Shawn. "We don't have enough evidence yet to arrest and charge Big G Gamboni for arranging the murder of his wife and her lover, but we're working on it. We need to clear the Gambonis out of the

Witness Protection Program, so we have the budget to cover Eugenio Morelli and his family. We want Mrs. Morelli to be happy because we want Smoothie to continue cooperating. So far, he's proven to be a fountain of information. Interpol thinks he could help us bust other members of the mob's hit man network in Europe and chop off a few heads in the Sicilian mob too."

"Smoothie loved being the Vegas mob's fixer, now we'll see if he can make the transition to being our mob wrecking ball," said Wilson.

RAT REMORSE

Bernard "Bernie" Bunyan, the mob's front man for the Whitehorse Casino on the Las Vegas Strip was concerned. His best pit boss, Eugenio "Smoothie" Morelli, was off his game. Somehow, he and his crew had failed to spot and remove a Midwestern card counter named Clint David before he'd taken the house for $170,000 at a blackjack table and beat it back to Peoria.

"What the fuck, Smoothie? How far did you and your crew have your heads up your asses to let that yahoo farm boy scam us like that?"

"Geez, I'm sorry, boss. You can take it out of my

wages, and I'll take it out of the crew's hide. We were asleep at the switch. Truth is, I haven't slept much at all since the twins were born. I'm thinking of camping out here during the week, even if I gotta bed down on a roulette table."

The twins were the least of Smoothie's problems, of course.

"You guys might want to tell Agent Shawn to ease up on Smoothie's interrogations and give him a couple nights off," Lenny Birch told me on a phone call after he witnessed Bernie Bunyan reaming out Morelli.

"What do you mean? I thought he was singing like a canary. What's going on with him?" I asked.

"I think he's losing it because of all the pressure from the Bureau bleeding him for information on his mafioso connections and their operations," the undercover fed said. "He is working a full day at the Whitehorse, still doing some minor fixing jobs for the organization at night, and then Shawn and his boys are working him over when he should be sleeping or keeping his wife and kids happy. Of course, that's not possible because his old lady knows the Bureau plans on uprooting the whole family—if the mob doesn't figure out he's talking and kill them all before they've been tucked away somewhere."

SEPARATION ANXIETY

Agent Shawn had brought in a pair of good-cop, bad-cop FBI interrogators from the Bureau's DC headquarters to work on Smoothie. Special Agents Van McKinley and Charles Maloney were experienced in the persuasion arts. Both had advanced psychology degrees.

They put the screws to Morelli five nights a week for two weeks.

"We don't use physical torture because we don't have to," said Agent McKinley during initial discussions with Agent Shawn. "We can crawl inside his brain and mess with his mind so much that he'll wish we were torturing him."

"You don't have to break him down into a drooling zombie, guys," said Agent Shawn. "He's been cooperative for the most part. I just think he's freaked out about the impact of all this on his wife and kids."

The goal of the first five sessions with Morelli was to gather information relating to the hit-men-for-hire operation that Smoothie had used to connect

Gunnar with Fred Montgomery and at least three other murder-minded husbands.

The goal of the second five sessions was to gather information on the Las Vegas and Sicilian crime families based on Smoothie's wise guy affiliation since his Cicero childhood.

After completing all the sessions, the interrogators said Morelli might prove to be the mob mother lode of damning information.

"We've had to play hardball a few times, especially this week on the mob stuff, but Smoothie has come through with a lot of useful intelligence that we can leverage in our organized crime investigations here and in Italy," said Agent McKinley. "Your pit boss and fixer may need therapy after all we've put him through."

The designated "good cop" McKinley and his "bad cop" interrogation partner Maloney determined early in their meetings with Morelli that he'd been raised Catholic and educated by nuns and priests, so he was afflicted with all the typical neuroses and guilt that came with that upbringing. They used that as their wedge into Smoothie's psyche.

"I know you are Irish Catholic, so the psychological baggage is a little different for you than the

Italian Catholics, like Morelli, especially those who grew up in the mob," McKinley told Agent Shawn.

"What the hell are you talking about?" Shawn asked. "It's the same damned Roman Catholic Church for all of us. Fish sticks on Friday. Mass on Sunday."

"Not exactly," said Maloney. "In our interrogations with Mafiosos, we find they are the ultimate smorgasbord Catholics. They pick and choose which teachings of the church are convenient for them to follow and which don't work for their criminal lifestyle.

"Guys like Smoothie, for example, have no guilt over murdering their enemies, or even arranging hits on other people's enemies. Their God is the jealous, wrathful, and vengeful God. He's not the blue-eyed Irish version with little birds perched on his shoulders and a two-hundred-watt halo," the FBI interrogator said.

"When we sit down with guys like Smoothie, we can't use their Catholic guilt to get them to confess to crimes because they are convinced that God was a hit man too."

"So, you're telling me the mob Catholics don't have any of the usual guilt that the nuns and priests drummed into us in parochial school?" Shawn asked.

"That's the interesting thing about these guys, including Smoothie," McKinley said. "They don't have a bit of guilt about their criminal lives, but they have boatloads of guilt about their **family** lives. Smoothie is a cold-hearted bastard when it comes to beating up casino cheats or setting up murders, but he goes to pieces at the thought of doing anything that might hurt his wife and kids."

"He wants to be a good husband and father more than anything else. So that is the card we play when we want to get information out of guys like him," added Maloney. "It's worked perfectly with Morelli, but I'm a little worried Smoothie's gonna crash if we don't give him a break."

Agent Shawn made similar observations about the mob fixer's fragile mental state while briefing him on the next stage of their investigation.

"Your days of working at the Whitehorse Casino will be ending soon, Smoothie," said Agent Shawn. "Once we act upon the information you have given us, it won't take long for your mob buddies to connect the dots and figure out that we flipped you. Before that happens, we'll be putting you and your family in protective custody in a safe house under twenty-four-hour guard."

Morelli did not respond. His eyes were glazed over. The bags under them were sagging like deflated balloons. He looked like the "before" guy in a Sominex sleeping pill ad.

"Are you getting all this, Eugenio?" asked Agent Shawn, testing to see if his informant still remembered his given first name.

"Yeah, I guess, I'm just having a hard time processing all the shit you've thrown at me in the last two weeks," Morelli said. "I'm worried about my wife and kids. I'm worried about my bosses finding out that I've been talking to you. And I'm worried about waking up buried alive in an Indiana farm field."

"Yeah, I get that, but you need to pay attention or you really could end up as crop fertilizer," said the FBI agent.

He couldn't blame Smoothie. The interrogation team had turned his brain inside out. His lucrative life as a casino pit boss and mob fixer was over. He'd never make that kind of dough again. His family was about to be uprooted from their cozy suburban pool home for God knows where, courtesy of the Witness Protection Program.

"Is Peggy taking this hard?" Agent Shawn asked.

"Is the pope Catholic?" Smoothie replied. "Ever since you fed fucks showed up at Dr. Rossi's office, the love of my life has cried more than both twins put together. Neither of us can sleep unless we drink enough Chianti to pass out.

"And the worst has yet to come. She will be hysterical when the US Marshals guys tell her that she can't spend holidays with her parents anymore because the mob will probably monitor their activities in hopes of finding me, cutting off my dick, and sticking it down my throat," Smoothie said to Agent Shawn.

"Some guys would be happy never to see their in-laws again," the FBI agent said, trying to identify a bright side.

"Don't fucking remind me. Her old man may be a corporate guy, but he's mean as a snake. When he and his wife find out that they can't see their grandkids, oh, my God, they will frickin' track me down for the pleasure of skinning me alive."

"Aw, man, this too shall pass, Smoothie, I promise."

"Just fuckin' shoot me now, please!"

CHAPTER TWENTY

LADY DEATH

SUNDAY, SEPTEMBER 7, 1975

Well, this is certainly strange. It seems all I had to do to become extremely popular was retire.

Once again, former SAS Captain Laurence Haywood had picked up the **Sunday Times** during breakfast in his London flat overlooking the Thames, and, once again, after reading through the big stories of the day, he'd taken a quick look at the personal ads.

I don't know why I still do this, but even though I'm not looking for work anymore, I do find some of these personals to be amusing. Like this one seeking "fellow furverts from the furry fandom community for a yiffing party."

I wonder what the hell that is all about?

Haywood made a mental note to look up definitions for "furverts" and "yiffing" in case it ever came up in cocktail-party conversation.

Wouldn't want to seem unworldly, after all.

He was scanning down through the rest of the personals when a familiar tagline caught his eye.

Captain XX, please call Avi. This one's for you.

That was strange enough, given his retirement from contract services, but just the day before he'd been contacted by another "agent" offering an opportunity in a coded message in the same newspaper's help wanted ads.

Fire Damage Cleanup Services Sought. Please call Jenna. This is a highly challenging job.

Then, yet another agent he'd worked with had left a coded message on his answering machine later that morning.

"Please call Konrad. Old wounds require treatment by you and Mila."

Three messages for me? Three potential missions? All in the last couple days? What is this?

The third message was the most intriguing because very few people knew the significance of the name **Mila** for him.

That was the nickname he'd given his classic Mosin-Nagant sniper rifle modified for long-distance targets. He first became familiar with the Russian-made World War II rifle as part of his special sniper training with a covert black ops unit.

He'd been recruited for the unit, known as the Armory, because of his SAS experience. Only veterans of special forces were allowed. Their mission was to support Britain's Secret Intelligence Service, MI6, for duties including sanctioned assassinations, subversion, surveillance, reconnaissance, intelligence gathering, extractions, and other missions the government would never acknowledge, whether they failed or succeeded.

Haywood had explained the black ops unit in this way to a friend who'd been recruited after him: "Unlike Ian Fleming's James Bond character, most MI6 field operatives are more intellectuals and academics than combatants. We provide their muscle and military strength. Everything about our involvement was covert. The unit has no public name. We do not wear uniforms, civvies only. In fact, we have a clothing allowance because the missions range so widely. We must blend into our surroundings, whether assigned to an operation inside a foreign embassy, a brothel, or a bathhouse."

Because of its wide range of missions, the unit also recruited women military veterans, especially those trained in counterterrorism. The Captain's favorite sniper rifle was named for a woman he met while serving in the top secret unit, but she was not a member of it. She was his sniper trainer, and a World War II hero hailed around the world, except in Germany, where she had been among the Nazis' most feared enemies.

Mila Volkov was preparing to apply for medical school in Moscow when the Nazis invaded Russia in June of 1941, during World War II. Like most Russians of her generation, she had taken military training in elementary school that was required by the Communist Party. She had proven to be an excellent marksman and was invited to join a women's shooting club that competed with others across the country.

After the invasion, the top-ranked women were recruited to attend the Central Women's Sniper School. She was among nearly two thousand women to graduate during the war. Mila had hoped to serve as a medic in the Red Army; instead, she became its most decorated sniper.

"Before the Nazis invaded, Stalin felt women should serve in the military only as support staff, nurses, cooks, and clerks, but when the Germans destroyed much of the Russian Army forces in the first wave, the patriarchal attitude toward women changed," Major Volkov explained to Haywood and his fellow recruits at their unit's training facility on the RAF base in Hereford.

"They realized women were fit for the role of sniper because we had more patience in waiting for the perfect shot and, thanks to our anatomy, we could endure stress and cold better than most men," the major added.

"When the Nazi forces were bearing down on Moscow, they needed us to fight, and fight we did."

Haywood and the other new recruits in the black ops unit had already been briefed on Major Volkov's accomplishments. She was regarded as the best female sniper in history, with 309 confirmed kills, including thirty-six enemy snipers. This was even more remarkable because she served less than a full year of active combat.

She was severely wounded by shrapnel in the summer of 1942 and taken off active duty. Plastic surgery was required for wounds to her long forehead, prominent nose, and high cheekbones. The surgery somehow softened her once stern Slavic features and left her with a kinder, more feminine appearance.

When she recovered, Russia awarded her a gold star as a Hero of the Soviet Union and sent her on a propaganda tour of several Allied countries, including the United States where she was the first Soviet citizen invited to the White House.

"She dined with the Roosevelts. A folk song was written about her. This woman is a true hero, the real deal," said the unit's director of training in introducing Major Volkov to his prized recruits.

The former Russian soldier won over Haywood and the other British recruits with her confident bearing and humble manner, and especially her sharpshooting demonstrations on the rifle range, which had to be extended to accommodate her skills.

"You may have been told that the Nazi officers stopped wearing insignia of their rank on their uniforms because our snipers were selectively killing so many of them," Major Volkov said during her first demonstration. "I am here to tell you that this story is true, but it did not stop us from killing more of them. You could always identify a German officer by his arrogance, and we would aim for that."

The special forces veterans were particularly impressed with her shooting accuracy given that Major Volkov was still using a WWII-vintage Russian weapon.

"I know you all think this is an antique, and it is, just like me," she joked, though she was not yet fifty years old. "This is a 1932 model Mosin-Nagant, a .30 caliber bolt-action rifle with a five-round internal magazine. This basic model has been used by Russian forces since the 1890s when the tsar's army first began using it," she said.

The sniper modifications included a 3-5-power fixed-focus scope based on the German Zeiss optics, she explained. "If you know how to use it, the effective aimed fire range can exceed five hundred meters. If you are as experienced as I am, you can add at least another hundred meters to that. It is a simply constructed but powerful weapon with a kick that will bruise a soft shoulder. So if you are to rely on this rifle, you must be as tough as it is—and this rifle is nearly indestructible."

After training with an assortment of classic and more modern sniper rifles, the Captain came to favor Major Volkov's favorite weapon, the Mosin-Nagant, which he named "Mila" in her honor. They had bonded over coffee after early morning training sessions, at first, and later, on weekends when they would slip away from the base for dinner and wine. There was affection, but no romance between them at first.

Her scars were only the most visible wounds from her wartime experience, she said.

"I always hated that Nazis nicknamed me 'Lady Death,'" she told him. "You may find it difficult to understand, but while I am proud of my service and my skills as a sniper, I carry a great burden of guilt for all the lives I took, and for the grief afflicted upon their loved ones. That is why I rarely get more than a couple hours of sleep, and probably why I've consumed so much vodka and wine since the war ended," she told Captain Haywood.

Major Volkov was ten years older and outranked him, as she often reminded him. And so, he was deferential, glad to have her trust and friendship, wary of crossing the boundary for fear of offending her. On her final night at the RAF base, after she'd fulfilled her contract to train members of his unit, the major invited him to dinner and then to bed.

"I would have offered sooner, but I've put up so many barriers over the years," she said the next morning. "There was no opportunity during my military service, even if I had not shut down that part of my mind and body. Then, afterward, my long-repressed grief, guilt, and fears emerged and overwhelmed me."

Only in the last few years of training soldiers had she found some peace, losing herself in teaching them all the skills that had kept her alive in the hope that they, too, would survive.

"I hope you are never so haunted, my friend. Promise me that you will never take the lives of innocents. That is the only thing that has given me solace. It is enough of a burden to kill our enemies. You should never take pleasure in what we do. Those who kill for pleasure are not soldiers; they are psychopaths and sociopaths. Feeling remorse and sadness upon taking a life is a healthy sign that should not distract you from your duties. It is an indication that your humanity is still intact."

Other members of his training group noticed that Captain Haywood and Major Volkov were often together outside of the classroom and shooting range. When they learned that he'd named his sniper rifle for her, they gave Haywood no little grief.

"Mila? Seriously, how can you kill with a weapon named for a woman, and a Russian at that?"

"Just remember," he told his antagonists, "my Mila, like her namesake, is never to be taken lightly. For she is a killer and an avenger for all women who have been mistreated by the likes of you."

CHAPTER TWENTY-ONE

HIT MAN HIT

A. J. Alexander dreamed that a fire hose was blasting water beneath his hayloft "loft" apartment in the main barn of the Rocky Waters Stables & Equestrian Center. He woke up only upon realizing the sound was flowing from Tom-Tom, one of the Clydesdales used to pull the resort's Christmas sleigh. The stallion was unleashing a mighty stream of horse piss in his stall directly below.

Once the rank odor of Tom-Tom's torrential discharge reached the hayloft, A. J.'s girlfriend, Riley Nicholas, awakened alongside him.

"**Ewww!** Tom-Tom! What a stinking way to start the day. I wanted to sleep in. It's six-o'-fricking-clock in the morning."

"And it's a day off for both of us too. Remember?" said A. J., holding a pillow to his nose.

A. J. worked summers on the Rocky Waters Golf Course greenskeeping crew. He shifted to a job as a ski lift operator at the resort in winter. Riley summered as a cart girl on the golf course and wintered in the ski resort's business office. She'd started out working as a ski lift operator too, but after a day of standing in the snow, she decided she had an aversion to frostbite.

Both had graduated the previous spring from Colorado State University in Fort Collins. Riley had planned to go to law school in the fall, but then she'd met A. J. while hiking in Vail and decided to stay with him "to see where it goes."

A. J. graduated with a degree in criminal justice and had applied to join the US Forest Service but hadn't heard back yet. He'd been a linebacker on the CSU football team, a freshman walk-on who became a two-year starter, so he was confident he could handle the rigors of being a forest ranger.

"Grizzly bears aren't that much bigger than running backs, right?"

"Maybe if you're talking the SEC or the Big Ten," replied Riley, who was already honing her courtroom debate skills.

Both A. J. and Riley had the day off because of a special event at their resort.

"I heard my boss say it's a golf tournament for FBI agents from all over the country," said Riley. "Didn't you tell me you majored in criminal justice because you wanted to be an FBI agent?" she asked her boyfriend. "Maybe you should go to the course and hand out résumés."

"The FBI is hiring only people with law enforcement experience these days," said A. J. "Plus, my boss told us to stay away from the resort until Sunday night. He said we'd be fired if he caught us anywhere near the golf course. And besides, I have a plan for us on our free day."

"You don't say? What have you come up with, Mister Master Planner?"

"What do you say we go four-wheeling in the Jeep and head up to the Pioneer Cabin near Sarah's Falls just south of the golf and ski resorts. Bighorn Creek runs by the cabin and the trout fishing is awesome there. We could catch some fish, cook 'em up on a campfire, and then just do some lazing around."

"What exactly do you mean by 'lazing around'?" asked Riley with a sly smile.

"It means whatever we decide it means when we get up there," A. J. said.

An hour later they were inside the Pioneer Cabin, fishing poles parked on the porch, and doing some serious lazing around inside a sleeping bag.

Then they heard a distant gunshot and then the faint roar of a helicopter.

"Geez. It sounds like the FBI hackers couldn't shoot par, so they are shooting at each other," Riley said.

SLIPPING THE TRAP

Under Agent Shawn's direction, FBI Special Agent Davis Satterfield Jr. was chosen to play the fictitious wife-hating golfer Rogan "Lefty" O'Rourke because he had a three handicap and the walnut burl tan of a veteran golf pro. He also owned a set of custom-fit Ping irons and MacGregor woods, which saved the FBI the cost of renting a set for the fake golf tournament.

Agent Satterfield, posing as Lefty O'Rourke, left his Osprey Inn room at 7:30 a.m. Bruno Kleiss, a.k.a. Gunnar Rolf, watched him while hidden in a housekeeping closet. He recognized the husband who'd hired him from photographs provided in his briefing packet.

Bruno was wearing a room-service waiter uniform he'd swiped from the laundry. The hit man also had stolen a wheeled food cart from the supply room.

He had not bothered to bring a pot of hot coffee and a breakfast plate.

Mrs. O'Rourke won't be around to enjoy bacon and eggs because she will be eating lead. He chuckled to himself.

Bruno stashed the food cart in a custodian's closet and ran down the stairs to make sure O'Rourke left the hotel and headed for the pro shop next door. He then took the elevator back to the top floor, retrieved the food cart, and headed down the hallway toward O'Rourke's suite.

It was nearly 8:00 a.m., which was a serious problem from the FBI's point of view. Gunnar's packet of instructions had told him to take the food cart to the O'Rourke's suite at 9:00 a.m., but Bruno was on his own schedule. He'd been provided photographs of both the husband and his wife. Mrs. O'Rourke was a beauty. The photograph was taken on a beach. She was wearing a bikini and displaying a sexy, playful smile.

This target might be worth a little more of my time.

The enticing pose had been intentional. The FBI profilers described "Gunnar" as a predatory male, a woman hater, likely a victim of childhood abuse, compelled to punish women for their imagined sins.

The FBI profilers had advised Agent Shawn that the best bait for his trap for Gunnar should depict a beautiful woman in a sexy pose, which would trigger the killer's bloodlust.

Bruno took the bait, but he decided he could not wait for the designated time of his attack. His professional discipline had been eroding in recent years, and he'd found it increasingly difficult to stifle his worst impulses on assignments like this, especially if an attractive young woman came into his sights.

Maybe that bitch Mrs. O'Rourke will still be in bed in her slinky negligee if I show up early, and maybe I can have some fun before— or after—I kill her. What's the difference? Her husband wanted her dead. Sooner is better than later.

As Bruno pushed the food cart down the hallway toward the O'Rourke suite, Agent Shawn was settling into a chair in the hotel security video-monitoring center. He'd planned on taking at least an hour to get oriented and psyched up for the biggest bust of his career. Instead, he looked up at the security monitors and saw a hotel waiter with a food cart headed for the O'Rourke suite.

He yelled at the chief of Osprey Inn security, Martin Hickman, standing across the room. "Hey, Marty, is that one of the service staff? Or should I be worried?"

Hickman looked up at the screen.

"Oh, fucking fuck, you should be very worried because I don't recognize that guy—at all," he said.

As Bruno walked down the hall, he heard disturbing sounds from the rooms. Male voices, a lot of them, which would have been normal with a golf tournament underway, except the former special forces soldier and GSG 9 officer also heard the familiar sound of weapons being loaded and checked, and the rustle of armored vests being donned.

Agent Shawn sent out a two-way radio alert to his SWAT team members just as Bruno stepped in front of the door to the O'Rourke suite. The hit man heard doors opening up and down the hallway and did a quick calculation.

They probably left this room empty in case there would be shooting.

Before any of the SWAT team members could get a bead on him, Bruno had pulled his revolver from the food cart, shot the lock off the suite door, charged into the room, and opened the glass doors to the rear balcony.

There, he performed another rapid calculation.

A three-story drop could be risky, but not if I land on one of those.

There were four rows of Club Car golf carts lined side by side beneath the balcony. Each of the carts had a hard plastic roof.

Bruno climbed over the balcony railing, hung on for just a second, and then dropped down. He landed on a golf cart roof, which collapsed and dumped him onto the grass. In an instant, he was up and running like an Olympic sprinter.

"Jesus, that fucker is fast," yelled Special Agent Sam Mahon, the first SWAT team member to reach the suite's balcony. He saw Bruno run into the woods and took one shot, but then held his fire. There was too much activity in the area. They hadn't planned to clear it this early.

Mahon grabbed his two-way radio: "Target in flight, headed for the woods behind the hotel. Repeat. Target in flight, headed for the woods behind the Osprey Inn. He's armed and moving fast!"

The radio alert went out to all the SWAT team members at the resort, more than fifty of them, including the team manning the FBI helicopter.

"Get the bird in the air," Agent Shawn ordered.

Now, the plan had been to populate the golf course with FBI SWAT team members posing as golfers in the tournament. But the plan had to be changed when reality intervened. There just weren't **that** many FBI SWAT team members available for this operation, especially any who could pass as real golfers. As a result, the Bureau had been forced to bring in a lot of young, inexperienced guys. Most of them were still in the Academy. A few of them were just college recruits or interns.

The first six foursomes posing as golfers were already on the course playing along with the charade in case the hit man was doing early surveillance. One of the few actual SWAT team guys, Agent Satterfield, was posing as the husband who'd hired the hit man. He was putting for a birdie on the third hole when he heard the radio alert, which made him blow the putt.

"Well shit, the party's over, boys! Gunnar is on the run in the woods. Go! Go! Go!"

He and the other fake tournament players threw down their clubs, grabbed their weapons, jumped into their carts, and drove toward the woods just as the FBI chopper roared overhead, sweeping over the treetops in search of the fleeing hit man.

The Greg Norman–designed course followed the natural flow of the terrain. The groomed tees, fairways, and greens were tucked into rock cliffs and outcroppings and surrounded by thick stands of scrub oak, aspen, alders, lodgepole pines, pale blue spruces, and Douglas fir.

The FBI's motley crew scrambled to pursue Gunnar and drove across the smooth carpet of fairway without giving much thought to the very different type of terrain awaiting them in the woods. Many of them were from Midwestern states where you could drive a golf cart from one end to the next without hitting anything more than a cow pie or a gopher hole.

Once they'd crossed the tree line, nature reminded them they weren't in Kansas anymore—and their golf carts were not all-terrain vehicles.

"Whoa, slow down. Slow down!" yelled an intern from Wichita just before his golf cart launched off a buried boulder, throwing him full force into a sturdy aspen.

The other three cartloads of feds met with worse fates. They plunged into the woods in a close single-file formation. The first cart, driven by Agent Satterfield, an Illinois boy, crashed through thick undergrowth before plunging into a hidden ravine with a rock bottom. The two carts closely trailing had no time to brake and they, too, took the plunge, crashing into the first cart and each other as they tumbled into the deep ravine.

All the SWAT team members were ejected or leapt from the carts and landed on jagged rock and scrub trees. Their guns and rifles spewed into the woods around them. Agent Satterfield's leg was broken. His passenger, Agent Salvatore Recchi, smashed his hip replacement and was incapacitated. Agent Schuman's face collided with a lodgepole pine and was turned to pulp.

Only two of them managed to crawl out without assistance, find their weapons, and rejoin the others giving chase on foot. None of them had eyes on Bruno who had a head start and the advantage of years of training in special forces SERE courses (Survival, Evasion, Resistance, and Escape).

Unlike his pursuers, Bruno moved through the woods at a cautious but brisk pace, choosing the path of least resistance, alert for obstacles and treacherous gullies, trenches, and ravines. He'd wisely fled down-hill from the golf resort. A path to higher ground meant slower, tougher going, and less oxygen to breathe.

The valley below provided easier going, as well as more cover. The thick tree canopy and dense foliage would make it more difficult to get a shot at him, even for the SWAT team members in the FBI helicopter.

When the hit man found a mountain stream, he followed it, staying close to the tree line for cover, diving into the pine needles blanketing the forest floor whenever the chopper flew close to his position.

I need to find a vehicle. Surely there are homes or campgrounds along this stream.

After trekking three miles through the woods, Bruno saw a small log cabin ahead on the banks of the stream. It was an old structure, but well-maintained. There was smoke coming from its chimney.

Bruno slowed his pace and went deeper into the woods, circling to the other side of the cabin. A banged-up Jeep was parked next to it.

If that Jeep made it all the way up here, it can take me out.

Bruno crept up to the Jeep and looked to see if

there were keys inside. None were visible. He opened the driver's door to see if the keys were tucked into the visor or in a compartment.

"Hey, what are you doing? Get outta there!"

A large young man, bare-chested, wearing shorts and no shoes had come out the back door. He had no weapon, but he looked formidable in Bruno's assessment.

Muscular, a weightlifter and athlete, probably an American footballer judging from the surgical scars on his shoulder and knee, Bruno thought as he reached for the pistol in the holster tucked in the back of his pants.

A. J. turned to enter the cabin when he saw Bruno reach for his weapon, but he ran into Riley who'd come up behind him. He staggered backward just as Bruno fired, which saved him from being shot through the heart. The bullet entered just below his rib cage instead.

A. J. went down.

"Riley, run!" he screamed.

She froze instead. Bruno's pistol was pointed at her forehead. His vulpine eyes scanned first her face and then her body. She was wearing only a T-shirt.

"How would you like to come with me for a little ride down the mountain?" Bruno said, leering at her.

Riley took a roundhouse swing at his face, but Bruno grabbed her wrist and yanked her to the ground, standing over her.

"Where are the keys to this Jeep?" he demanded.

"In the cabin, on the table. Just take them. Leave her!" said A. J. as he struggled to stand.

Bruno aimed the pistol at A. J.'s chest.

Riley screamed and kicked at Bruno's legs, causing him to pause just an instant.

The sound of a distant rifle shot echoed through the woods. It came a split-second after Bruno's head exploded into fragments and a red mist. The 7.62 mm 7N1 sniper rifle cartridge left his crumpled body with only a mangled jawbone and portions of a tongue hanging from his neck.

Riley rushed to A. J.

Minutes later, the FBI descended, emerging from the woods, and a helicopter bearing the FBI insignia landed with more heavily armed men.

"Did you shoot him?" Agent Shawn asked Riley and then A. J. as a medic attended to his wound.

The young couple, suffering from shock, could only shake their heads in unison.

Agent Shawn whirled and asked the SWAT team members circled around them.

"Who the hell shot him?"

"It wasn't any of us, sir," replied their leader.

CHAPTER TWENTY-TWO

BOULDER

The Captain, Laurence Haywood, took his time on the drive from Vail to Boulder. His lunch date at the Sink, Lily's favorite campus dive, wasn't until twelve thirty, and the fall colors along the highway were spectacular. He was feeling reflective and unusually content, maybe even buoyant, about the prospect of finally retiring, for good this time.

Maybe I should stay in Boulder for a few weeks, catch up with Lily, meet her friends, and enjoy this weather. I could even buy a home here. Maybe see if Kay is willing to leave her fancy London friends and retire to the mountains with me. Why not? I certainly can afford it. I dare say, I've never been so well compensated for a single

hit. And this target was one I would have taken out for free. Hell, I might even have paid for the opportunity to kill that demonic wanker.

There would never be a paper trail to show who had paid the Captain to track and kill Bruno outside Vail. None of the three entities were aware that two others had paid him as well. All three clients wanted Bruno eliminated for the same reason. He was no longer a disciplined assassin who could be relied upon to fulfill an assignment without leaving a trace. He had become a loose cannon, abducting, torturing, and murdering random women even while on assignment.

The Cosa Nostra contracted with the Captain because they did not want to be linked to any of Bruno's kills, those they'd ordered or those he'd murdered for his own deviant pleasure.

The GSG 9 assigned the Captain because Bruno, once one of their best men, had become a serial killer, and thus, a threat to the organization's reputation. The third client had come from a referral. A former SAS colleague who'd become a private security contractor had passed on to Haywood a bid for his services from Madam Steinau, the operator of a Copenhagen brothel.

She knew the client as "Herr Hecht," but when she showed a photograph taken by a camera hidden in her brothel, the Captain recognized Bruno.

"He murdered, molested, and cut up the body of one of my girls, after promising he would not harm her, and for that, he must die," she told the Captain.

Madam Steinau said Herr Hecht had brutalized and killed a prostitute named Roma just hours before departing for Vail.

"My sources in the intelligence world tell me this evil man, whatever his name, has a contract to kill someone there," she'd said. "They also tell me that it may be a trap set by American law enforcement. I don't trust that anyone can capture him, or kill him. If they do, fine. But you will be my insurance, Captain. I want you to make sure he does not leave that mountain alive."

His contacts with the Cosa Nostra and GSG 9 had told him the same thing.

"I have no doubt that Bruno will smell their trap and escape them," said the GSG 9 representative. "He is far too skillful for the Americans, unless they get lucky. And I don't think they are that lucky. We trust that you can get the job done, Captain. Go to Vail.

Decide where Bruno will flee when he escapes the trap. Set up with your sniper rifle and take him out."

A week before Bruno arrived, the Captain had traveled to Vail. He wore a prosthetic nose and a dark-haired wig so he could surveil the golf resort in advance. He'd seen FBI agents meeting at the resort and listened as they plotted their strategy in the bar. He also had walked the golf course and then rented an ATV to find the optimum sniper position.

I've had the same training as Bruno. If I was fleeing from the FBI SWAT team, I would enter the woods and follow this stream, hoping to find a vehicle and maybe a hostage.

Haywood had found the vacant Pioneer Cabin, which seemed to be a favorite place for fishermen judging from the trout heads and tails drawing flies in the trash can outside.

If nothing else, he will pause here to drink from the well before heading to the busy campground just downriver.

There was a ridge of boulders above a waterfall that created a pool in a sharp bend in the stream a few hundred yards from the cabin. The best position on the ridge was farther from the cabin than he might have wished for, but still within Mila's range.

That is where he set up and waited on the designated day for Bruno's hit on the golfer's wife.

The Captain had learned the specifics of the FBI's plan not from his eavesdropping at the resort but from the contents of a large envelope left under the door at the cheap roadside motel ten miles outside Vail where he had taken a room.

The unmarked envelope included a copy of the materials Bruno had been given for the hit, with all the details and photographs. The only message on it was handwritten on a piece of stationary bearing the logo of the Rocky Waters Golf and Ski Resort. It said, "If he enters your sights, take your shot. No one will come for you."

Bruno seems to have made many more enemies since he stuck his knife into my leg years ago.

The Captain was set up on the ridge with his upgraded Mosin-Nagant sniper rifle, awaiting Bruno, when the young couple pulled up in the old Jeep. He thought about warning them away but decided that might get complicated. The Jeep would attract Bruno's attention if he made it to the cabin.

The Captain fretted about the safety of the couple as they fished the stream, laughed, and flirted. When they went into the cabin, his concern did not diminish. The young man had taken the Jeep's keys with him, and Bruno would want those. He also would want the young woman.

At the sound of a gunshot and the roar of the FBI helicopter, the Captain resolved to shoot Bruno at first sighting, hopefully before he could engage with the couple inside the cabin. But the fleeing hit man had circled to the back of the cabin and come up behind the Jeep. The Captain did not have a clear shot until Bruno moved to the rear door of the cabin and prepared to shoot the young man. Thankfully, the girl was a fighter and distracted him for a split second. That was all the Captain needed.

I wish I could have taken the shot earlier, but I had to wait for him to step away from the Jeep and into my line of fire. I am sure the young man will survive, and I am very happy that the young woman, and others like my Lily who might have become Bruno's victims, will never be threatened by him again.

This one was for all of them, and for Major Volkov, Mila, who taught me that seven hundred yards is not an unreasonable distance when armed with her training and her favorite weapon.

CHAPTER TWENTY-THREE

FACIAL RECOGNITION

MONDAY, DECEMBER 1, 1975

Wilson walked out of the chief's office grinning like he'd just won a John Wayne look-alike contest.

"Hey, Kenda, the Bureau sent over a photograph along with some of the evidence they've dug up on the Montgomery killer since he was taken out," he said. "The FBI joined their German counterparts on a search of the guy's farmhouse hideaway in Garmisch. They found records of wire transfers and phone calls that will help us link him to Fred Montgomery and the other husband suspects on our list."

"What's the asshole's name?"

"He had a dozen fake passports, so no one can say

for sure, but the name that keeps popping up as maybe legit is Bruno Kleiss," Wilson said. "It appears he was in the German special forces before joining their federal police unit, GSG 9, and, later, became a mercenary and contract killer. Interpol thinks he might be the serial killer who targeted prostitutes across Europe."

"Prostitutes?" I said. "Let me see his photograph, please."

I am very good with faces. If I see you just once, I will remember you. And when I saw the face of Bruno, I remembered him too.

"I saw this guy buying a Heckler and Koch submachine gun at the gun show in Castle Rock when we went there to bust Buckler," I said. "I'll bet he bought the wadcutter ammo there too. And that is where you and I got the same admission stamp found on the hand by that couple's dog up on Gold Camp Road."

"Holy shit. That was the day before Mrs. Montgomery was murdered," said Wilson.

"Yeah, I knew there was something wrong with that guy," I said. "Now we know he was loading up on guns and ammo to kill Kathryn Montgomery, but her scumbag husband won't ever get his hands on her money."

Fred Montgomery had continued to deny that he hired Bruno to kill his wife, but the judge and jury did not believe him. We tagged him on charges for solicitation to commit first-degree murder, and first-degree murder. The trial was a three-ring circus. To make the case that Montgomery had tapped into a global network of hit men, many of whom were highly trained former special forces soldiers, the prosecutors subpoenaed members of the Las Vegas mob and Sicilian Cosa Nostra, not to mention a small army of former Navy SEALs, Green Berets, GSG-9, and SAS members who had served as mercenaries and private security guards around the world.

Then the prosecutors brought in expert witnesses from the FBI, CIA, MI6, and Interpol to enlighten the jurors further on how government-trained elite soldiers went rogue and marketed their services as hit men around the world.

The Birch brothers, Doug and Lenny, also testified, and they proved to be the star witnesses. Their big mugs were plastered on front pages and television news reports from New York City to Paris, France, and beyond. They landed a book and movie deal and announced that they will use the proceeds to open the first gambling casino and bingo hall owned and operated by Native Americans.

JUSTICE SERVED

The guilty verdict forced Fred Montgomery to pay off his greatest debt—the one he owed society—by serving a sentence of life in prison without parole. The other three husbands who had hired killers were also convicted and received long prison terms.

Luca De Vecchio was tried and convicted in federal court since he'd ordered a contract hit on his wife while they were in the Witness Protection Program. I'm sure "Big G" received a warm reception in prison from all the mob members he'd ratted out.

Wilson and I took great satisfaction in sending Fred Montgomery and the others to prison, but we were even more thrilled that Bruno Kleiss, the sadist and psychopath who had tortured and killed so many innocent women, did not make it to a trial or to prison. He suffered the fate he deserved outside that Colorado mountain cabin when his demented, deviant brain was splattered into a bloody gore that slid down the door of that brave kid's Jeep and stained the ground below it a dark red.

In my view, that made all things right in the world, at least for a moment.

ACKNOWLEDGMENTS

As always, I would like to acknowledge all the dedicated law enforcement professionals and first responders I've been fortunate to know and respect over the years. For this book, I particularly want to thank my son, Daniel J. Kenda, CMDR, US Navy (Ret.), for providing his input and expertise in weaponry. Also, thanks again to my wordsmith Wes Smith for helping me on this, our third book together and our first dive into fiction as partners in crime. The best part of our collaborations over the years is that we have become good friends.

ABOUT THE AUTHOR

Lt. Joe Kenda spent twenty-one years chasing killers as a homicide detective and commander of the major crimes unit in Colorado Springs. After retiring from law enforcement, he starred in **Homicide Hunter: Lt. Joe Kenda**, an American true-crime documentary series that ran for nine seasons on the Investigation Discovery network and was aired in sixty-nine countries and territories worldwide. **Homicide Hunter** airs on Investigation Discovery, the #1 true crime channel, which is available in more than 80 million homes. **All Is Not Forgiven** is his first novel.